Names Have Power

Tim's Magic Voice Makes A Harem

Doctor MC, Mad Scientist

doctor_m_c@hotmail.com

Ὑπό Τῷ "Ηλιῷ

HYPO TO HELIO BOOKS

Houston

Paperback ISBN: 978-1-938293-01-6
Ebook ISBN: 978-1-938293-07-8

Front-cover render-art by: Doug Sturk
Author-photo render-art by: Doug Sturk

Contact Doctor MC, Mad Scientist at:
doctor_m_c AT hotmail DOT com

This is a work of fiction. Names, characters, places, and incidents are the product of the author's imagination, and any resemblance to actual persons, living or dead, business establishments, events, or locales is entirely coincidental.

All sexually active characters are eighteen or older.

HYPO TO HELIO BOOKS
2427 Clearbrook Drive
Missouri City, Texas 77489-6061

Chapter 1
I See A Head-On Collision

Call me Timothy. Or Tim. But please don't call me "Big Tim"—that was my father, not me. Absolutely do not call me "Little Tim"—that was cute when Dad and I were first doing commercials, but it's not cute now. And I don't need a crutch and I don't play ukulele, so "Tiny Tim" is out.

Everything changed on the evening after my father's funeral. I'd always thought of my father as "the happy bear," and bears don't eat healthy; it was some cholesterol problem that had killed him. So two days earlier, at the age of 27, I'd became heir to Dad's Ford dealership. The truth is, I'd rather have had my father around for another thirty years, but such is life. Anyway, after listening to one more car dealer make one more insincere expression of sympathy, I had to get out of the house! I told my mother that I needed to go for a walk.

Standing by the front door was 22-year-old Susan Cooper, my father's executive secretary. From the looks of things, Mike Brown, the general manager, was trying to hit on her. Again. I guess he liked a challenge, and the Ice Bitch was certainly a challenge! Anyway, when I brushed by her, she turned her back on Mike to face me, and she demanded, "Where are you going?"

"Out, I need to get out."

"You're leaving? That's rude! People here want to talk to you."

"Are you one of them?"

"That remark is borderline inappropriate behavior, Mister Hanson."

"The people who genuinely mourn my father's death, they're talking to my mother. The men who seek *me* out are checking-out the fresh meat."

She crossed her arms. "Still, it's rude to leave now."

"Tell you what, Susan: After *your* father dies, *then* you come advise me about funeral etiquette."

She drew herself up straight. "I am *Ms.* Cooper to you, Mr. Hanson. I am a professional, and I deserve and expect to be treated professionally by you, both *on* and *off* the jobsite!"

I glared at her. I'd met her for the first time, five years ago, when I was a college senior, and she was an eighteen-year-old, just-graduated, new-hire with big breasts and shiny brunette hair. She'd treated me like a cockroach on the day she'd met me, and her attitude had never improved.

"Whatever. I'm gone," I said to Susan.

I stepped outside, into the night. Upset, I wandered through the subdivision. After a time, I was gazing at the stars, at what turned out to be a stop-signed intersection. I was looking up when I heard the roaring of approaching engines and the screeching of tires. I looked down just in time to see, right in front of me, the head-on between the sports car (a current-year Nissan 350Z, red) and the SUV (last year's Ford Expedition XLT, black).

By all the laws of physics, the sports car should have been the bigger mess; and the sports car's driver, a corpse. But that red car was only lightly damaged (except for the driver door flung open on impact). The driver unfastened her shoulder harness and stepped out of the car. I found myself facing a goddess with a cut cheek.

She was big-breasted. I like big-breasted. She was tall. I like tall. She was slim and muscle-toned, she was tan, she had the face of a catwalk model, she had the lips of a porn actress, she was blond, she had a peaches-and-cream complexion, et cetera, et cetera, yada-yada-yada. Even her *ears* were perfect!

"Please," she said, "help me, sir, I've lost a contact. *Please* help me find it." She had the voice of a phone-sex operator—why was I not surprised?

My hormones started vibrating like a tuning fork. But at that moment I realized: The SUV was too still, too quiet.

When I tore my eyes away from the goddess to look at the SUV, I noticed that the inside of its windshield was red, and getting redder. Somebody needed help!

I pulled out my cel then; but strangely, it said "No Signal." It was up to *me* to rescue the SUV people.

I shrugged at the woman, then moved to rush around the back of her car. "Those people need help. I can help you later."

"Do you have a flashlight? Matches? Anything for light? I'd *really, really* appreciate it." Jeez, she was talking about *a flashlight*, and that voice was giving me a boner!

By now I was five feet away from the SUV driver door. A bit of blue, down low, caught my eye. At my feet lay a blue butane lighter. I could rush back and hand the lighter to Goddess, and be a hero! Maybe I could work that up to a date with her? Or I could toss the lighter to her—*that* might be worth a kiss on the cheek.

But even a split-second spent fooling around with Goddess's lighter would mean still more delay before the SUV people got help. "Sorry," I said over my shoulder, as I came to the black SUV's driver door.

The driver was a balding man in his forties, still in his shoulder harness. I saw and heard no passengers. The man wore a white shirt, and a blue tie with little white polka dots. Both shirt and tie were blood-soaked.

The driver's neck was spurting blood at the windshield! Through the ruined side window, I heard him mumble, "Help. Me."

I cut my hand (I didn't notice till later), opening the car door. I reached for his neck injury, and the blood spurted against my hand like a spurt-spurt lawn sprinkler turned up full. When I pressed down, to try to stop the flow of blood, I cut my hand again—on glass embedded in his skin. Still, I pressed down, and felt hot liquid run down my hand and arm, and drip off my elbow.

Which meant, I could not stop his blood loss. He would die while I supposedly was helping him! I felt like shit.

"Okay? Me?" he murmured.

Oh jeez, what was I supposed to tell him? Then I thought of what I'd want to hear if I were in his situation, and the answer was clear: *the truth.* "I'm sorry, sir, but I can't call 911 and I can't stop your bleeding."

"I. Die."

"Yes, sir, I'm truly sorry. I suggest you get right with your God."

He snapped his head around to eye me—*where did he get the energy?* He then spoke the strangest "last words" that I ever expect to hear—

"That blonde, she's so beautiful, isn't she? But always, you chose the dying man," he said. Then he closed his eyes, and his chin dropped to his chest.

"Oh, ick! You've got blood on you," I heard the blonde say.

I decided in that instant that the blonde wasn't nearly so beautiful as I'd thought. I looked at her, through the rising radiator steam that the SUV was making. I intended to tell the blonde to show some compassion, but before I spoke, she disappeared.

Then vanished her red sports car. Then gone: the black SUV. Then no more blue butane lighter.

Standing next to me was the dead SUV driver. But his skin and clothing was bloodless somehow. His eyes were open again, and they were looking at me, as his body changed. His mousy brown hair turned black, his bald parts filled in with black hair, and his skin? It turned *golden.* He looked like the father of that dead girl in *Goldfinger.* His clothing disappeared, shrank, or recolored until he was wearing only a black loincloth. He waved a hand, and the cuts on my hand were healed. Another wave of his hand, and I was as clean of blood as he.

"Who *are* you?" I demanded. "What just happened?"

He clapped me on the back—and for a dead man, he was strong! "I will not tell you my true name, Timothy Richard Hanson, for names have power. But *what* I am is an ancient god who has no more worshippers, and who has wandered the earth since before the Time of the Carpenter."

"And what just happened?"

"It's a test, a test I've given to *this* man or *that* man for 562 years. In the test's original form, the older man and the young beauty were seemingly the victims of highwaymen. The details differ, but the test has remained the same." The golden god eyed me. "And for 562 years, until this hour, every man has failed this test."

He went silent then, to let me figure it out. And soon, I did: "The other men helped the beauty who clearly needed no help, hoping for sex with her, and they neglected the dying man nearby."

He nodded.

I thought some more, and sighed. "She was *hot*."

He smiled. "As well she should be. I made a reading of your brain, mortal. Men rate every body part of every woman they ever see, and Tiffany was magicked from all of your Ten-parts. She was *designed* to 'push all your buttons.' "

"So what happens now, since I passed your test?"

"You get rewarded, just like in the children's stories that your Grandmother Priscilla read to you. But I doubt that you want a goose that lays gold eggs."

"Yeah, the IRS would ask rude questions."

"I decided long ago, what would be a suitable reward if I ever found a man such as you. I copy to you one of my godly powers, Timothy Hanson. The power I give you would be *dangerous*, if given to those lesser men."

So saying, a ball of blue fire shot out of his left eye, as a red fireball shot out of his right eye. The fireballs came together to form purple fire, which continued to move toward me; but the purple fireball streaked down below my jaw. I felt something hit my voice box. The sensation was warm and tingly.

"The effects are not reversible, so use my gift wisely," the golden god said. "Remember, *names have power*."

"*Wait!* What did you—?"

The god smiled, then vanished.

The next morning, I woke up thinking that I had dreamed all of it. Until I noticed that on my left hand, I had dried blood under my fingernails.

Chapter 2
Telling Off Susan

This was my first day to come to the dealership, ready to own it. Even so, it felt wrong to park in "my" space—I felt like I were trespassing on Dad's spot. I walked past Ms. Cooper into my inner office; she, as usual, was dressed like a Vassar grad who was working at a brokerage firm.

My father had held a Morning Meeting of senior managers, every day at eight; I continued that tradition. So five minutes after I arrived for work, gathered in my inner office were Mike, my horn-dog general sales manager; Albert, the always-serious service manager; Bobby, the parts manager; Betty Jane, the finance manager; Kathy, former student-council president and now my sales manager—and of course Ms. Cooper, who was taking notes.

I read from my scribblings on a legal pad. "First, it's time to film a new sales ad. But I'm not going to shoot a standard 'We're having a sale' ad—"

"Why not?" asked Kathy. "After all, this weekend we *are* having a sale."

"Oh, I'll *mention* the sale. But business-as-usual seems—well, ghoulish right now. So what I'm thinking for the ad is that I talk, but the visual is old video of Big Tim. Ms. Cooper, please go through our old video and film, and find ads that show my father's nature."

"Certainly, Mr. Hanson," Susan said. Surprisingly, she didn't get all huffy at being asked to do hours of extra work.

"Second thing," I said. "I've hired an accountant from Detroit to audit the dealership. Please cooperate with him. This is *not* a reflection on any of you."

Mike raised a hand in a "stop" gesture. "So why do it, why have an audit?"

"I love my father, but he was never a good man for record-keeping. His records here are pathetic."

Mike frowned. "I feel like my honor is being questioned. I've kept a lot of those records, and if you're thinking, Tim, that those records are no good, then maybe you and I can't work together."

"Are you telling me that if this auditor walks in, you're walking out?" I said, eyebrows raised.

"Please, let it be so," Susan murmured.

Mike nodded, looking martyrish. "I feel that my honor is at stake."

"And *I* feel that I have a right to know the finances of my new dealership. Michael, we *will* be audited; accept that and go on."

I expected Mike to keep arguing then. But instead he said, "Sure, you need to start with clean books. I saw that, but I was hoping I could make you think you owed me a favor. I guess I can live with an auditor." His face and body were relaxed now, and he looked 100 percent sincere.

That statement sounded fishy for a hundred reasons. But I let it pass—why argue with someone who's just agreed with you?

I turned my eyes back to the legal pad. The rest of the stuff written on it was routine. The Morning Meeting went another fifteen minutes.

After Albert and Kathy left, Mike came over to me, leaned over, and murmured, "Make plans for tonight at the Nimfo Club. You, me, and Albert. My treat!" Then Mike left my office.

Which put me alone with the Ice Princess.

I hadn't slept well, and now that I was coming down from the adrenaline high of my first-ever Morning Meeting as the Boss, I was feeling sleepy. I didn't think things through, and so I looked at Susan and said, "Get me a cup of coffee, please. I'm desperate."

She glared at me. "No, Mister Hanson, I will not. My agreement with your father was that coffee was *not*—"

"Oh, cut the crap. He's dead, so you could claim that he promised you a million dollars a year."

"Don't be ridiculous," she said with haughty voice. "But he and I *did* have an agreement about coffee, and *you* are breaking it. This is almost Inappropriate Behavior."

For five years I'd put up with her treating me like a cockroach, but *no way* was I going to *pay her a salary* to treat me like a cockroach! I came *thisclose* to firing her that instant, even knowing that she'd try to sue the pants off me afterward.

Instead, I growled, "Susan Gloria Cooper, if I want to 'Inappropriate Behavior' you, I'll ask you to live in my house with other women and to serve in my harem. Believe me, short of me asking you to join my harem, nothing I do with you is inappropriate behavior, you got that?"

"Yes, Mister Hanson, I—"

I went for broke, I was that mad. "You don't work for my father now, you work for me. Unless you quit. And maybe you should."

"Now just a minute—"

"Your attitude stinks. We are in the 'friendliness' business, my queen." I gestured toward the showroom. "The men and women on the floor, they have to be friendly and helpful. Say it's Thursday night and the salesperson is way behind quota, because it's been raining all week? Too bad, he has to be friendly and helpful to the customer who does walk in. Say the customer has never heard of soap or a toothbrush? The salesperson still has to be friendly and helpful. You wouldn't last *five minutes* out on the floor!"

"So? I am not a sales whore here, I have a *good* job," Susan replied.

"You don't think *what you're doing* is sales? When a customer says, 'I want to talk to the dealer,' and he winds up on the other side of your desk, or talking to you on the phone? If you treat *him* like you treat *me*, he's going to storm out of here and tell everyone he can talk to, 'Don't buy a car from Tim Hanson Ford.' "

"I don't treat customers like that," she said stiffly.

"So why do you treat *me* like that?" I yelled. Before she could speak, I said, "Susan Cooper, you shall be friendly and helpful around me from now on, so that you'll be by-god in practice when you talk to customers. And Susan Gloria Cooper, the friendlier you are to me, the more helpful you are to me, the better. Got me?"

She smiled at me. *Smiled!* She said, "You're right, and I thank you for showing me how to do my job better."

Something is weird here, I thought. But what I said to my secretary was, "Then I'm glad we had this talk, Ms. Cooper. I don't want to fire you."

"Oh please, Mr. Hanson, you know my name. Call me Susan, or better yet, I'm Susie. How do you prefer the cream and sugar in your coffee?"

At 3 p.m., Susan had film and videotape ready to show me. As I was looking at old images of my father (and of me), Susan asked, "Mr. Hanson? Suppose I gave you a thousand dollars of my money, and a list of all my clothing sizes. I took you to a mall, and asked you to buy work clothes for me. What would you buy me?"

"My lawyer would advise me not to answer that question. No comment."

"Please, Mr. Hanson, I'm sure that you answering my question isn't sexual harassment. Please answer, I need to know."

I thought, *Let's yank her chain and see if she's really changed her attitude.* Aloud I said, "I'd buy dresses that would show off your chest. Plus really sexy blouse-skirt combos. All with a hemline that is well above the knee. Plus the highest heels you could walk in, a garter belt, and sexy stockings." To make the joke even more jokey, I added, "Ribbons for your hair, and a nail-salon gift certificate for a full set of top-grade long nails."

"No pants? No pantyhose?"

"Hey, if I'm spending my evening buying you clothes, instead of watching ESPN? No pants, no pantyhose, forget it."

I was expecting Susan to be screaming at me by now, threatening lawsuits and EEOC complaints, loudly enough that she could be heard in Hawaii. Instead, she nodded. "I see. When would I wear this clothing? Casual Friday?"

"*What?* I give up my hypothetical evening to buy you clothes for work, and you wear them one day a week? That's not friendly."

She gasped. "You're right, that is so wrong!" She squared her shoulders and looked at me. "I will go shopping tonight so that after today, I'm dressed friendly. Garters, stockings, and very high heels, the whole shebang, every day."

"Don't forget the long nails and the hair ribbon," I said. "Every day."

Susan eyed me. "You can count on me, Mr. Hanson."

This whole talk had turned strange. Why hadn't Susan realized I was joking? Why wasn't she mad at me and lecturing me about "inappropriate behavior," like in olden days?

Mike and Albert came to my office at five, to take me to the gentleman's club. As they were walking me out, Susan asked, "Mr. Hanson, Mr. Hanson! How long should my fingernails be?"

"Say what?" I said.

"If I go to a nail salon to get long nails, and the nail tech asks, 'How long?', what should I say?"

Much of my conversation with Susan today had been strange, and this conversation was even more strange. Worse, Mike was giving me a look that said, *What's going on? Are you fucking the Ice Princess?* So, annoyed with her, I answered, "Hell, Susan, make the length what's wildly impractical, and that makes every guy think you're easy."

Susan nodded her head, then Mike dragged me to his car.

Chapter 3
I Learn Strippers' Secrets

Albert, Mike, and I had been celebrating at the Nimfo Club for an hour when the night turned strange.

Mike gestured a circle to mean all the strippers. "See one you like?"

I pointed to a big-breasted blonde. "Her, definitely. Platinuma."

"Oh yeah," Mike said, "with that body she'd be fun for a few fucks, for sure."

"Well, I'd want to date her too, not just fuck her."

Mike snorted. " 'Date'? As in, 'Buy her dinner and chocolates and roses and shit'? Hell, Tim, all the women here are whores—except for the dykes, of course. Just hand 'em folding cash and you won't need to worry, 'Will she or won't she?' *Fuck* the roses!"

"I hear you, Mike. But I'd still like to date her," I said, and I meant it. Yes, she was gorgeous—gorgeous babes were apparently standard equipment at the Nimfo Club. But there was another thing: When she danced, sometimes there would show sadness in her eyes—but then a second or two later, that sadness would be masked again. She was *human*.

Mike said, "Tim, I'm gonna do you a favor." He got up, walked over to Sad-Eyes Girl, and basically *dragged* her to our table.

Up close, I saw that under filmy lingerie, she had enormous tits (swear to God, they looked real). She also had long legs, platinum-blond hair (probably fake), and pale blue eyes (which I hoped weren't contacts). She turned her eyes on me and—I blanked out.

Lesson One of selling cars is: Learn the customer's name, then say the customer's name. Lesson Two of selling cars is: Say the customer's name often. But when the sad stripper looked at me, *I couldn't remember what to call her!*

So I said, "Please, tell me your name."

She leaned down and murmured in my ear, "My real name is Sarah Elizabeth Buchanan." She stood up and, at regular volume, then said, "But here I'm 'Platinuma.' "

"Thank you, Sarah—I mean Platinuma."

Mike whooped. "Damn, Tim, you are da man! Strippers *never* give out their real names."

Albert nodded. "I thought giving out your name was against club policy, Platinuma."

Sarah/Platinuma shrugged. "He looks like I can trust him."

Mike said, " 'Trust him'? Platinuma, or Sarah, take a look at Tim Hanson here. He's the new owner of Tim Hanson Ford."

She looked at me with funeral-face. "I liked your dad. He was funny to watch on TV."

"Hey, no sadness tonight," Mike said, "the funeral's over! Platinuma, tonight you be *very, very* nice to Tim here, because now he's a rich car dealer."

I nodded and smiled shyly at her. "Yes, Sarah Elizabeth Buchanan, from this moment on, I'm your boyfriend. Well, for tonight just pretend to be, okay Platinuma?"

She gave me a warm smile. "Not a problem. You're cute."

Sarah started moving her body to the music, as she eyed me and smiled. At first I thought she was going to give me a standard table dance, but then she came even closer. Within seconds, she was grinding her pussy against my leg.

"Isn't that against club rules?" I heard Albert say.

Mike said, "*Supposed* to be. Damn, she looks hot!"

Sarah's dancer legs had power. Sarah could hold herself up so that her pussy lips would just brush the cloth of my pants, moving down my leg, then she would lightly move back the other direction, which again made my pants caress her pussy lips. Her nipples got hard, and she bit her lip.

Down my leg—rub. Up my leg—rub. Down my leg, up my leg—rub, rub. Sarah dragged her pussy all the way up my leg, then she grabbed my hand. "Touch me," she murmured into my ear. "Please. I'm wet for you."

Boy howdy, she was. To a thump-thump bass beat, I stroked her clit and slowly pistoned her with a finger, and she shook like she was in an earthquake. I'll swear she had an orgasm every fifteen seconds. If the sound system hadn't been so loud, I think her moans would have gotten us both arrested.

Suddenly she stood up, grabbed my other hand, pulled me to my feet, and said "C'mon!"

"Where we going?"

She nodded toward a part of the room enclosed with dark-tinted glass. "V.I.P. Area."

"*Damn*, Tim!" I heard Mike laugh, as Sarah dragged me away as fast as her stiletto-heeled feet permitted. "She thinks Ford dealers are rich," Mike added.

Inside the V.I.P. Area, we were lucky to find an empty booth. (Hell, we were lucky to *see* an empty booth. The place was a cave with loud music.) Sarah insisted that I order a drink.

"What kind of drink?"

"Doesn't matter, but club rules are, you got to be invited by a dancer to come to the V.I.P. Area, and you got to order a fresh drink to stay here."

So when the cocktail waitress came around, I ordered a Coke. (I'd already reached my two-beer limit.) I had to explain to the waitress that "Mike Brown" would be paying for the drink, but fortunately(?) she knew who Mike Brown was. When I tried to buy Sarah a drink, she turned it down. "It would be only ginger ale," she explained, "regardless of what they charged you for."

The cocktail waitress left. Sarah said, "Good, now the rules are met." She groped in the dark for my belt, which she then unfastened. Sarah was on her knees, and had my cock exposed to the dark air, before I realized what was going on.

I can't recall now, what her cocksucking technique was like. But I recall very well that I had never before enjoyed a woman so *hungry* to suck me off and to swallow me. When the cocktail waitress returned with my Coke, Sarah didn't pause an instant. Sarah stopped milking me only after I patted her head and then I shook her shoulders, trying to get her attention. (The cocktail waitress, meanwhile, had stepped around Sarah and had continued with her business, which told me a lot about life in the V.I.P. Area.)

By the time I was no longer seeing stars, and had put my cock back in my pants, Sarah was sitting next to me in the booth. I kissed her. I couldn't see her face, but I think she was surprised. "Thank you very much," I said. "I'm grateful, Sarah."

The cocktail waitress was walking by at that moment. Sarah grabbed her leg and said, "Hey Betsy, do you have a cocktail napkin in your pocket? Let me borrow a pen and your flashlight." Betsy gave those things to Sarah, who said, "Turn your head, Betsy, so you can't tell Yuri anything."

Sarah then wrote her phone number on the cocktail napkin, which she jammed into my pants pocket. *Whoa!*

After Betsy the cocktail waitress left, Sarah said to me, "I've given you an X-rated dance, I've sucked you off, I stopped you from buying me a watered-down drink, and I've given you my phone number. How else can I make your night wonderful?"

I put my arm around her shoulders. Damn, her skin felt nice. "Hmm, you told me your real name, which I guess is supposed to be secret. What are other secrets of this club that customers aren't supposed to know?"

Sarah pointed through the glass to a gorgeous redhead dancing the pole. "That's Sunset. Hair color is real, tits are fake. No surprise, right? But that pretty pussy, that's fake too."

"No shit?"

"Hm-hmm. The manager doesn't care, but Sunset's legal name is still Robert."

"Wait, I'm confused. Isn't the surgeries the expensive part, and going to name-change court the cheap part?"

"Sunset's sugar-daddy got arrested for embezzlement," Sarah replied. She shrugged (I think) in the darkness.

Sarah continued, "Going the other way, there's Gothika." Sarah pointed to a black-haired woman, currently table-dancing, who was wearing black lipstick, black nail polish, a skimpy black bikini, and black leather high-heeled boots. Each cup of Gothika's bra was covered with a picture of a flaming skull. Instead of filmy lingerie to cover her stripper clothing, Gothika was wearing a knee-length black-leather coat. Gothika's tits were gigantic, beyond even the pretense of being real.

Sarah continued, "Gothika, it turns out, is honey blond, the only true blonde here. She is known here in the V.I.P. Area as a true champion of cocksucking; I'm told that her deep-throat is wondrous. That pink Lexus in the parking lot? She paid for that *herself, cash*, six months after she started here. But she parties only with girls."

"So what is Gothika's real name? Bertha? Zelda?"

"Are you ready for this? It's *Ashley*. And Gothika says that Ashleys drive only pink cars."

"She sounds fascinating. I'd like to meet her."

Yes, Reader, I know Gothika was a lesbian whore. But I had to admire someone who made choices and took chances and pursued goals, rather than drifting through life, and who succeeded in life as a result of taking charge of her future. No big car dealer got that way by winning the lottery.

After I said that I'd like to meet Gothika, Sarah was silent for several seconds. When she spoke, her voice sounded resigned. "Well, I have to leave in two minutes to dance my set, but stay here and I'll bring Gothika when I come back."

Sarah danced on stage for three songs. When somebody gave her a cash tip, she looked at him and gave him a dick-hardening smile. But most of the time she was looking in my direction, even though the V.I.P. Area's dark glass meant that Sarah couldn't see my face.

True to her promise, when Sarah returned to the V.I.P. Area, she brought Ashley/Gothika with her. "This is Tim Hanson the car dealer," Sarah said to the black-haired stripper. "He wants one of *your* blowjobs."

"How much money do you have on you, Tim?" Gothika asked.

"Whoa, halt, stop," I said. "I said only that I wanted to *meet* you, Gothika, not *get a blowjob* from you."

"You are big-league shitting me now. I'm gone," Gothika said.

"Ashley, I'm telling you the truth, I'd love to talk to you for several hours over wine and find out how your mind works, and Sarah's already told me that I'm not getting in your pants! As for your blowjob—believe me, Ashley, I'm curious about it, and I'd love to receive it. But I won't ask you for it. Number one, Sarah has just given me a world-class blowjob. Number two, Mike Brown made me lock my wallet in his glove compartment. Number three, since you're really good at giving head, Mike probably doesn't have cash enough to cover your fee."

"It was 'world-class'? Oh honey," Sarah said.

I thought, *"Honey"?*

Gothika laughed. "Damn, you're the first nice man I've met since eighth grade, and Sarah already claims you." Gothika turned to Sarah. "How much time since you blew him? Half-hour, at least?"

"At least."

"He's recovered," Gothika said. So saying, she dropped to her knees, and then *Ashley/Gothika* unfastened my belt.

Meanwhile, I was pulling Sarah's head down to my face. As Ashley was sliding her mouth down my dick, I was kissing Sarah's lips. Sarah kissed me like she meant it.

Sarah had been passionate in her cocksucking. Ashley sucked me the same way that an ace body-and-paint man hammered out a dent: Every second, she was thinking about what she was doing, and planning what to do next. The results of Ashley's thinking and planning were wondrous indeed: Whether she was sucking the base of my cock, tonguing my wrinkled spot, slurping my head, or tonguing my dick hole, every moment was perfect. The blowjob was as intense as it could possibly be, without ever being *too* intense—it was what a blowjob was *meant* to be.

Mike, Albert, and I were headed for the Nimfo Club's front door. Mike said, "I have to say, Boss, you're a cheap date. Your cover charge, then two bottles of beer and a Coke, that's all I bought you? Shit, I once dated a girl who was planning to enter a convent, and *she* drank more than that. Guy, I had all these five-dollar bills for you to tip the girls with, and you never used any of them. Don't bother telling me that you had fun."

As Mike stopped talking, Gothika strode up to me, pressed a cocktail napkin into my hand, grabbed my head between her hands, and gave me an eyeball-melting kiss. In my ear she murmured, "You won't get to fuck me. I won't let you lick me. But who knows where wine and conversation will lead?"

"*Fuck* me," Mike said.

"To tears," Albert added.

Chapter 4
Susan Has Changed

The next morning I walked into my outer office, and already at her desk was Susan. At least, I *thought* it was Susan. *What the hell?*

She stood up when I entered, and she seemed much taller. Then she walked around the desk, and I found out *why* she seemed taller: killer high heels. Which went perfectly with her sexpot outfit. "Do I look friendly enough?" she asked.

I thought that maybe she was being sarcastic. But no, I realized, she was *nervous*, not sarcastic. *Holy shit, she really wants me to like how she looks*, I thought.

"Do you look friendly enough?" I repeated. I picked my words carefully: "You look like you just came from a party." I didn't add, *A party at the Playboy Mansion.*

"But that's good, right? Parties are friendly. So everything's okay?"

Other than this woody that your tits are giving me, all is fine.

Truth be told, she wasn't *quite* outrageous enough for me to send her home to change. And now she sure was nice to look at! But there *was* one thing—

"Susan, when I talked about your fingernails, I meant half-inch at the longest. Inch-long nails are just *too* impractical for working in an office."

She looked horrified. "Oh, Mr. Hanson, I'm so sorry I misunderstood you! I'll take care of that tonight, promise. But please, call me 'Susie.' 'Susie' is friendlier, don't you think?"

"No problem, Susie."

"Um, I'm sorry about my hair."

"Your hair?" Susie's hair was long, dark brown, thick, and shiny—after her chest, her hair was Susie's best feature. Today that dark-brown hair was pulled into a bun that was ringed with a chocolate-brown hair ribbon.

Susie touched her beribboned hair. "I ran out of time, Mr. Hanson, I swear. Everyone knows that blondes are friendly, but with all the clothes shopping I did last night, and the nail salon, I didn't have time to dye my hair! I'll do it tonight, promise."

"Susie, you don't need to dye your hair blond."

"I know I don't *need* to, but blondes are friendly."

As I walked through the door to my inner office, I thought, *I caused this somehow, my Power did this. But I have no idea what exactly I did!*

Before I had sat down, there was a knock on the door. I called "Enter!" and Susan stepped in. She put a cup of coffee on my desk, and turned to leave; but at the door she stopped and turned around. She said, "Mr. Hanson? I've been wondering: Why are men obsessed with harems? You don't see *women* wishing that they lived with seven horny *guys*."

I said, "I don't know why other men are obsessed with harems, but I know why harems excite *me*."

"Go on."

"When I was fifteen, my best friend and I were looking at one of the *Playboys* that his dad had. And in there was a picture of a sultan, with a turban and beard, and he's sitting on pillows. And in the room with him were about twenty young women—all of them hot, and all looking at him like each girl wanted to f—to have sex with him. And they weren't wearing anything but rings on their fingers, and rings on their toes, and each girl was wearing a transparent veil on her face. And one girl was feeding the man grapes, and another girl was lying on her stomach, sucking—uh, pleasuring the sultan. And that picture was sexier than anything I'd ever seen or imagined. And so whenever anyone says 'harem', this is what I think of."

Most men would think it weird to be discussing harems with their young, stacked secretary. But for me, the entire last twenty-four hours had been weird—this was just one more little weird thing. Which reminded me—I sipped the coffee that the former feminazi had brought me.

"Coffee okay?" Susie asked nervously.

"It's great, Susie. You remembered how I like it."

Hearing that, she visibly relaxed. "Anyway, thanks for explaining about harems and all."

"You're welcome, Susie."

The door that hot-dressed Susie was standing next to, had just opened. It was Mike, first to arrive for the Morning Meeting. He looked my secretary up and down and said, "I *like* the new look, Susie. You look great!"

Susan turned to eye him as she stood straight, her queenly manner back in full. "I'm still 'Ms. Cooper' to *you*, Mr. Brown."

My second Morning Meeting as the boss was strange.

The women managers, Kathy and Betty Jane, clearly were offended and confused. They were offended by Susie's outfit, but they were also confused whose idea it was to wear it. Kathy and Betty Jane had known Susan for five years, and couldn't imagine her dressing like a slut, just because she'd been ordered to; but Kathy and Betty Jane had known me even longer than that, and knew that I would never give such an order. So how was it that "Ms. Cooper" was dressed this way?

(I'm glad that neither Kathy or Betty Jane asked *me* that, because I sure as hell didn't have an answer!)

Mike, Albert, and Bobby had a difficult time, of course, keeping their minds on task, and I often saw a man squirming in his chair. I understood why: I had a titanium boner myself.

Susan played the Ice Princess for everyone but me. But when *I* spoke to her, she acted like a tail-wagging puppy. This raised eyebrows (among other body parts). Meanwhile, even when Susan was behaving like the Ice Princess, she remained dressed like a soft-porn secretary.

I introduced my people to Mr. Sanderville, the accountant from Detroit. Mike looked unhappy to see him, but said nothing. Mr. Sanderville never noticed Mike's reaction—Sanderville's eyes were on Susan's breasts at the time.

After the Morning Meeting, Mr. Sanderville stayed in my inner office, going through paperwork there. While he was there, I phoned Sarah and set up a date for the first evening she was free (which was next Monday, unfortunately). Sarah seemed very glad when I called, and very warm over the phone.

Finally, about three in the afternoon, Sanderville and his laptop headed to the Service Department. As soon as Mr. Sanderville walked out, Susie walked in. Correction: she *sashayed* in. "I thought he'd *never* leave," she growled.

"Huh?"

She moved toward me, her eyes on mine the whole time, those fuck-me heels making her ass move delightfully. "Mr. Hanson, I can't be *very friendly* and *very helpful* with him in the room."

I saw where this was going. "Susie—"

"Nothing's more friendly than a blowjob, Mr. Hanson. And if you're stressed, Mr. Hanson—and with your job, you can't help but *be* stressed—"

"Susie—"

"—then nothing's more helpful than a blowjob."

She knelt.

"Susie, if I let you blow me at work, this is *wildly* inappropriate behavior."

Her hands were working my zipper. "No, Mr. Hanson, I *know* this isn't inappropriate behavior. And I would be a bad secretary if I didn't suck you off at least once a day." She looked me in the eyes, my cock just an inch from her lips. "If I don't suck you off, I'm *bad*. I deserve *punishment*."

"Susie—"

She dropped the sex-kitten face for a nervous look. "I've only sucked cock once, Mr. Hanson. And then I tried to stop it as soon as possible. So it probably won't be good today. But if you let me suck you off every day, soon I'll make it good for you. Promise." Susie then gave me another sex-kitten smile, and grabbed my cock with her mouth.

"Susie, stop."

She ignored me. *Oh man, that feels good.*

"Susie, stop. I mean it."

She still ignored me. And then I found out, even a teeth-scraping blowjob is addictive—I couldn't make myself say *Stop* a third time.

A half-hour later, Susie had sucked me and had swallowed me, and now she stood up, kissed me on the cheek, and sashayed to her desk. It occurred to me that before yesterday, I'd never received an under-table or under-desk blowjob—and now I'd gotten *three* in under twenty-four hours. *I wish I could figure out what I did to make this happen!*

———

When I walked into my outer office the next morning, Susie greeted me with a kiss. Her fingernails were shorter, but still of porn-actress length; and she wore a blue ribbon in her long, honey-blond hair. You win some, you lose some. (Not that I *minded* honey-blond hair.)

Yesterday, as a brunette, she looked like a soft-porn secretary. Today as a red-lipsticked blonde, she was definitely hardcore, and I was definitely hard.

When I walked in, the time being ten minutes before the Morning Meeting, Susie had been surfing the Internet. Boy howdy, I was surprised when I saw her current page: "Lola Lush-Lips Explains: How To Suck Cock."

After the Morning Meeting broke up, Susie remained in my office. I couldn't talk her out of sucking me off, and then she demonstrated that she indeed had learned a few things from Lola Lush-Lips.

Blowjobs at work, I decided, are nice to get.

Chapter 5
Deborah Makes A Deal

That afternoon, Mr. Sanderville made his report. His news was not good.

"Mr. Hanson, there is $177,482.36 that your dealership should have, that I can't account for. The specifics are detailed here." He laid a folder on my desk.

"Well, I told you how my father was like, at keeping records."

Mr. Sanderville eyed me. "In at least one case, it might be more than that." He laid a second folder on my desk. "In April 2006 this dealership sold a 2004 Corvette for fifteen hundred dollars."

"*Fifteen hundred*? Wow, some junkyard guy got it cheap."

"It wasn't sold to a salvager, but to a regular customer, Deborah something. She put five hundred down, and financed the rest over twelve months."

I stared at him. "A two-year-old Corvette was sold for fifteen hundred bucks as a regular used-car sale?"

"Yes, and while there is a notation on the contract, 'Car is totaled,' there is no body-shop paperwork to prove such."

"Holy shit," I said.

I wrote Mr. Sanderville a check, then I walked him out to his car. Then I rushed back to my office and the Corvette folder.

Within seconds, I'd dropped two flags on the play.

Deborah Denise Parker had been a 23-year-old dancer at Club Physique when she had bought the Corvette, with income listed as forty-seven thousand. I doubted that she had gotten such a low price through great haggling.

The approving sales manager's signature? It should have been Kathy's. Instead, I saw the scrawl of Mike Brown. Who signed as finance manager, Betty Jane? Nope, Mike. Who wrote "Car is totaled"? That was Mike's handwriting.

I phoned my service manager. After pleasantries, Albert was asking me, "So Tim, you hooked up with Gothika yet?"

"Not yet, but soon. Anyway, Albert, I want you to recall back to April 2006. Tell me everything about a red Corvette, since you probably handled it."

"I know just the car you mean. Hold on." The next thing I heard was you're-on-hold music.

Soon Albert was back on the phone. "The Corvette was brought to us on April 12, its tag was EATDST, its VIN was—"

"What was wrong with the car? How did we get it?"

"The real thing wrong with it was the high insurance payments. The owner, Harold S. Brenner, was a fifty-two-year guy who changed his mind about owning a Babe Magnet. He told me, 'I want an unsexy car now, so I'm buying Ford.' "

"How about body damage? How about mechanically?"

"Body damage was car dings, and some white on the fender. It had 56,784.2 miles on it, and the AC compressor had gone kaput."

"So it was drivable. Sellable."

" 'Sellable'? Mr. Hanson, I went to Mike and I asked, 'How much for the car?' And I would've signed the nastiest finance contract that Betty Jane ever cooked up. But Mike told me, 'We already have a buyer.' "

Oh shit, I thought.

At five o'clock I was in the showroom, waiting and able to see everything, when Mike got into his car and drove off the lot.

I strolled over to Betty Jane's office, then chitchatted with her as she logged-off and put on her coat. As soon as Betty Jane was gone, I told Hank, the Assistant Finance Manager, to pull up the current address of Deborah the Corvette-driving stripper. Six minutes after Mike drove off the lot, so did I.

Deborah Parker lived ten miles from the dealership. Her apartment complex was gated, but I punched in 5-0-0-0 as the gate code, and I was in. The complex had prosperous tenants: Cars were late-model, the buildings showed good paint, and the landscaping was fancy. I parked my car near (but not *too* near) her building, and walked around.

I was driving a demo car, of course, with identical "Tim Hanson Ford" paper rectangles where the license plates were supposed to go. Near to Deborah's apartment door, I discovered another "Tim Hanson Ford" demo car, its hood being hot to the touch. Two spaces over from that car was the red Corvette. The Vehicle Identification Number (or as much of it as I could remember) in Mr. Sanderville's folder matched the VIN of this Corvette.

The Corvette's front was banged up somewhat, so a headlight was busted. But other than this, the car had never been in an accident.

To make sure of that, I gave the car a thorough examination. I looked at every inch of that car, and often I ran my hands over it.

Which set the car alarm off. Other than my ears hurting, the car alarm didn't bother me. If a cop showed up, I had Mr. Sanderville's Corvette folder resting on the dash of my car.

I was squatting down, running a hand along the passenger-side door, when I heard an angry woman's voice behind me. "Hey! HEY YOU, GET AWAY FROM MY CAR!"

I heard male feet running toward me, and Mike's voice saying, "Yeah, fucker, you better—"

I stood up and turned to face him. "I better *what*, Mike? Say, who's your body shop? For a 'totaled' car, this Corvette looks great."

Mike put on a winning smile, even as his face turned white. "Tim, buddy, it's not what it looks—"

Enough. I said, "Michael Brown, Deborah Parker, take me inside. We have much to discuss."

Either it was my righteous anger, or maybe it was my Power? In any case, Deborah invited me into her apartment. She even offered me coffee. Mike sat on her couch and looked wretched.

A woman can't look truly sexy when she's worried about going to jail. And Deborah was no longer a fresh-faced beauty of twenty-three. But she still was tall, with very long hair. Her hair was that color that's too dark to be red, and too red to be brunette. And either the dye job was very recent, or I was seeing her natural hair color. Her eyes were brownish green, and she had Katherine Hepburn cheekbones. She moved like a panther, when she didn't know I was watching her. (When she *knew* I was watching her, she made nervous gestures and her voice trembled.) Her tits were definitely fake, or else she'd won the Tit Lottery in junior high.

Debbie handed me a cup and saucer, and sat down on the couch, facing me. She sat a foot away from Mike.

Mike started to say something; I raised a hand. I said, "If by five tomorrow, either of you hand me a check for forty-three thousand dollars, you two won't go to prison. The check must be a cashier's check, made out to 'Tim Hanson Ford,' and it must be given *to me personally.*"

Mike said, "That's more than it bluebooked for."

I glared at him. "I figured-in six percent simple interest since April 2006. The forty-three is nonnegotiable; don't even ask."

I stood up and walked toward the kitchen. "Talk it over," I said.

They didn't talk long. They walked into the kitchen and Deborah told me, "We don't have it. We don't *begin* to have it." She was in tears.

" 'Don't have it'?" I said. I turned to Mike. "My dealership is short 177 grand. Tell us, Michael Brown, how much of that is *your* doing? Besides the Corvette, I mean."

"Sixty thou, maybe seventy. Your dad never noticed."

Deborah turned on him. "You stole seventy thousand dollars, and you can't spend it on keeping us out of prison?"

Mike sighed. "It got spent long ago—"

"On other strippers?"

Mike looked at me. "What about my job?"

"What about it?" I said to him. To both of them I said, "Here's your chance to be creative: Make me an offer. *But*, Michael Brown, Deborah Parker, whatever offer you make, if I agree to it, I expect you to keep the deal completely." Then I eyed Mike. "And if we reach a deal, I'll ask Betty Jane to write it up."

"Well, I suppose I can let Payroll take three hundred a month out of my check," Mike said, with the tone of someone sacrificing much. He was also working an Assumed Close on me.

"No deal," I said. Let the clown try to figure out whether I was saying No to his money offer, his assumption that he would still be on my payroll after today, or both.

"Mr. Hanson," Deborah said to me, with an edge to her voice, "didn't Mike take you to a strip club a few days ago? What club did you go to?"

"Debbie, baby," Mike said, "right now we have—"

I couldn't figure out what was going on with those two, so I answered honestly, "Mike took me to the Nimfo Club."

She slapped Mike, hard. Then she turned to me and said, "Mr. Hanson, you said to be 'creative.' You said to make you an offer, right? So here's my offer: I become your devoted sex slave and servant girl. Whatever money I earn, you get. You want sex, just order me. You want your floor scrubbed, order me. Home-cooked meals, ditto."

"For how long?" I asked.

"Goddammit, Debbie!" said Mike. "You are talking total pervert shit here."

Angry Deborah said to me, "I've talked for a while about putting in an app at the Nimfo Club. But Mike *Shit*brown here kept telling me, 'That place has liquor violations, and health-code violations, they deal coke in the parking lot, the city's about to close it down.' And now I find out he was all hot and heavy with some redhead named Sunset?"

"Debbie babe, she's not special—"

"Oh, shut up, Mike," Deborah said.

Then Deborah calmed herself, and again spoke to me: "As for the sex-slave stuff, it's for as long as you feel is fair—Mike says you're honest. Everything I have is yours, while I'm your slave. Well, except that I keep title to the Corvette."

Deborah fell silent. She and Mike looked at me.

My first thought was, *This is a joke.* But Deborah looked too serious for me to keep that idea.

My second thought was, *This is an agreement I can't ask Betty Jane to write up, Deborah must know that. I bet she'll try to welsh.* But if Deborah was working a con on me, it was fooling Mike, too.

The fact was, I'd come to Deborah's apartment not expecting to collect the forty-three grand, and I'd already decided I wouldn't let these two off the hook for anything less. So now I had two choices: sex-enslavement of Deborah (which *might* work out), or jailing Mike and Deborah.

If she's going to welsh, best to find out now. I said to her, "Mike and I are going to drive our cars back to the dealership, and then I'll return here, after Mike and I take care of some administrative stuff. Deborah, I accept your offer; and as soon as I walk in your door again, your enslavement begins."

She gulped, then nodded.

Back at the dealership, I collected Mike's demo-car keys, his general-manager keys, and his dealership credit card; got him to fill out (in my office, not his) all the paperwork that fired dealership general managers have to fill out; and then Hank and I watched Mike clean out his desk. Then I made Mike turn his back on his computer, and I changed his computer password.

Right after that, I got in my demo car and I headed for Deborah's apartment.

I don't know how Mike got home later. Bus, or taxi, or friend-as-chauffeur, or walked? *Who cares?* was my attitude—the lowlife had robbed my *dad*!

Firing a general manager takes time, and so it was awhile after I'd left Deborah's apartment complex, before I returned. I was shocked to find the red Corvette still around; I'd expected her to skip on me. I walked to the door of Deborah's apartment; I knocked. I had no idea what to expect.

Deborah answered the door.

Chapter 6
Slave Deborah

I walked to the door of Deborah's apartment; I knocked.

Deborah answered the door.

She was wearing green high-cut panties, a green transparent baby-doll teddy, and green platform heels. Her red-brunette hair was pinned up, and she sported dangling green-stone earrings. She looked *hot*.

She stood there, looking at me for several seconds; she said nothing. Then she squared her shoulders and stepped back. Still looking at me, Deborah said, "I invite you to come in, sir."

I was looking right back at her, and so I was looking at her face when I walked through the door. As I passed the threshold, she acted startled by something, then her whole body language changed.

She dropped to her knees, and wrapped her arms around my legs. "This slave loves you, Master!" Her face glowed like the sun.

If I hadn't met the SUV Driver, I'd think that Deborah was pulling a prank on me. But the last few days had taught me caution. "*Why* do you love me, Deborah?"

"Because Deborah promised to be your *devoted* sex slave and servant girl, Master. This slave's life now is to pleasure your eyes, pleasure your cock, and to obey you till you release me."

"Hoo boy."

What would *you* do if you suddenly got a hot stripper sex slave? Uh-huh, I thought so. What *I* did was to tell her to bring me her photo albums and yearbooks.

Even knowing that somehow I was magically changing people, I had totally not expected to *own* Deborah. But within a minute of Deborah dropping to her knees, I resolved that I would not hurt her physically, emotionally, or financially. But to absolutely make sure of that, I had to know what kind of person Deborah had been, before her enslavement.

An hour later, she was pointing to a swimsuit picture from 2005. ". . .And as soon as it did not hurt for Deborah to touch her new breasts, she walked into Club Physique. Deborah has worked for Club Physique ever since." Deborah got a thought: "Does Master wish for this slave to quit work there?"

"Huh. I'll need to decide that, won't I?"

Deborah turned a photo-album page. I saw a picture of Deborah and Mike in late 2005; the couple looked happy and sexy. I tapped the photo and asked, "How is it that you and Mike stayed together for so long?"

"He said such nice things to Deborah, and he brought Deborah flowers. He made Deborah feel like the most beautiful woman in the world."

"Okay, and what's the other half of that? The *Mike* half?"

Deborah smiled proudly. "This slave practices tricks with her pussy muscles, and this slave knows how to give two-hour teaser blowjobs. Or perhaps what Mike liked is that Deborah figured out how to give handjobs in a movie theater and never get caught."

I decided at that moment that I could look at the rest of Deborah's photo albums later.

Two minutes later, I was thinking, *Jeez, she's wet!*

And oh, since you're wondering: She wasn't lying about that blowjob stuff, and that pussy-muscles brag wasn't bullshit either.

Chapter 7
I Make A Big Mistake

It was the morning after I had fired Mike; also, the morning after Deborah had become my sex slave. Perhaps reading my face well, nobody at the Morning Meeting asked why Mike was no longer with us. I informed the group that I would soon promote one of them to Mike's job; in the meantime, I was acting general sales manager. (Which meant, no more sitting in my office for the next day or two.)

After the Morning Meeting, I remained in my inner office, intending to stay only a few minutes more. But Susie had other plans. Short of smacking Susie across the room (which I was *not* going to do), I couldn't stop her from dropping her mouth onto my cock. Sometime later, Susie swallowed my cum, stood up, kissed me on the cheek, and sashayed to the door and her desk beyond.

I stayed in my chair, realizing that I needed to face my responsibility.

To summarize: In the last four days, the Ice Princess had become my eager porn-fantasy secretary, two strippers had given me blowjobs and phone numbers, and a third stripper had become my devoted sex slave. I know I'm likable, but I couldn't believe that I'd made this happen just with my wit, good looks, and natural charm.

The golden god had given me a gift, and had said to "use it wisely"—which meant that I could control it. But clearly it worked even when I *didn't* control it. I had changed Susie, Sarah/Platinuma, Ashley/Gothika, and Deborah without trying to.

I tried to recall everything I'd done since talking to the god, to try to see a pattern. But searching my memory was a waste of time, for my memory had too many holes in it. *Damn*, I was frustrated!

"Timothy Richard Hanson," I said, "you somehow better *know* exactly what your Power has done, and you better *know* what to say to women in the future to make your Power work some certain way, or else you might really *hurt* somebody."

I felt something *click* in my brain. I thought, *Good God, somehow I've just worked my Power on myself!*

I walked out of my office. I strolled through the showroom, the inventory lot, the service bays, and the parts counter, all the time imperfectly recalling the last few days in my head.

I wondered again why Susie kept insisting on sucking me off, not stopping when I told her to stop. What was up with that? But then somehow I *knew* that it was because my Power wasn't being invoked then.

Recalling my night at the Nimfo Club, somehow I knew—without knowing how I knew—that when I started talking to Gothika, my Power had not kicked in, so that she thought I was bullshitting her; *but* shortly after, my Power kicked in, and Gothika got convinced I wanted to be her friend and nothing more.

In fact, the same Power-on, Power-off thing had happened with Sarah/"Platinuma"—

Fuck. Damnation. Shit, shit, shit.

I was Sarah's boyfriend now. Not a pretend-boyfriend, and not a one-night boyfriend, I'm the guy whom she now loved and she now fucked. She'd sucked me off in the Nimfo Club not because that's what sluts do, but because that's what girlfriends do.

———

I had run back to my office and, once I shut the door, I pulled out my cel phone and called Sarah. I forgot that she went to bed late and it was still early. She answered the phone in a sleepy voice. I said, "Oh, I'm sorry that I woke—"

"That's okay, lover," she said. "I'd rather lose sleep to talk to you, than be awake for anyone else."

I heard the faint sound of a crying baby. I said, "You have to get up anyway, to take care of your child."

She yawned. "I don't have kids. That's Shelley's little boy you hear. I'm sleeping on her couch."

"Um, don't you have an apartment?"

"Isn't safe anymore. After you called me two days ago to set up our date, I finally called up Duke and told him: He and I were done, I was seeing someone else. The night before last, when I got off work, I got a feeling. I asked George—bouncer, ex-military, he's huge—to walk me to my car. Outside, there was Duke. So now I have big bruises, but I'm not in the hospital, thank the Lord."

"I'm sorry about your bruises."

"You are so sweet. If you were here, I'd let you kiss them and make them better."

"Um, right. Listen, I'd better let you go back to sleep."

Sarah yawned again. "Wish you were here, honey. I'd cuddle you, and then I know I'd sleep like a log." Sarah's voice got sexy: "Or else I'd start a party, and then we'd *both* wake up."

As I put my cel phone back in my pocket, I thought, *What have I done?*

The door opened, and Susie walked in. "You okay? I heard you were on your cel." Susie's face got that sex-kitten look. "Mr. Hanson, you look stressed."

The words slipped out: "Susan," I said, "not now. Try later."

"I got you, you have to work. But remember, if your work gets stressful—I'm here to *help* you." She smiled at me, and started to leave.

"Susan, tell me: Have you stolen anything from the dealership, or cheated the dealership, since you started here?"

"Yes, Mr. Hanson. I've always written '8:00' on my timesheet, even when I've come in late. I've taken home two nifty pens, a black Ford t-shirt, and a pad of sticky notes. Please, Mr. Hanson, don't fire me."

I said, "I forgive you, Susan." She beamed as brightly as a beauty-contest winner, and then went back to her desk, happy enough to sing (quietly).

I followed her out of my inner office—it was time to walk my property and to work the General Sales Manager's job.

I got a thought, and stopped by Susie's desk as she was taking her seat. The golden god had told me that changes to people's minds were irreversible, but surely there were ways around that. As a test, I said, "Susie, your hair ribbon?"

"Yes, what about it?"

"From now on, Susan, don't wear a hair ribbon anymore."

The weird thing was, I had a hard time saying that sentence to Susie. Part of my own brain was fighting me, sending me a feeling of *I shouldn't be saying this!* Truly, forbidding Susie from wearing her hair ribbon was as hard to say as reciting porn-movie dialogue to my Great-Aunt Hannah would have been.

But less than a second had passed since I told Susie not to wear a hair ribbon. Now she said, "Mr. Hanson, I—"

My cel phone gave its text-message beep. I pulled out my phone, glanced at the display, and told Susie, "Have any questions, we'll talk later." I rushed off.

The text message was about a lawyer in the Service Department. He believed that his scheduled court appearance entitled him to head-of-the-line privileges for repair. I said to him, "Mr. Hollings, Edward, I'm sorry but. . .," and then I reminded him that *If I did it for you, then I'd have to do it for everybody, and then where would I be?* was a time-honored legal principle that he should be familiar with. Mr. Hollings calmed down immediately, without me needing to cut the price. Amazing, huh?

As I strolled around the dealership after that crisis, I asked every employee the same dishonesty-question that I'd asked Susie. I uncovered a salesman who regularly finagled his commissions higher, and a Parts man who evaporated F-150 parts to put on his truck. These two people I fired.

Lesser thefts I forgave, which made many of my employees truly happy (thanks to my Power).

I came to believe that only Mike had embezzled serious money, though there was still tens of thousands of dollars unaccounted for. I guess my father *really was* that sloppy in his bookkeeping. (Or else my father had caught a lot of crooks working for him, and had fired them so quietly that not even his own son got told why.)

Walking through the showroom, seeing the salesmen in their tiny offices trying to close customers, it occurred to me: my Power could make me the biggest car dealer in the city! All I'd have to do was say the magic words to each and every customer, and Tim Hanson Ford would have a 100 percent closing rate!

But if I did that, I would be a thief. Correction: I'd be something much worse than a thief, something evil.

My cel phone rang. It was Kathy. "Hey, Kath, what do you need?" I asked.

"Mr. Hanson? I'm at Susan's desk. Come here quick, she's babbling about her hair ribbon. She's freaking me out!"

I burst in the door of my outer office to find Susie sobbing while hugging Kathy. Susie's left hand was pressed against Kathy's back, and Susie's right hand clutched her hair ribbon in a fist. Between sobs, Susie was saying, ". . .have to wear the ribbon, but he told me not to wear the ribbon. But I have to wear the ribbon, but he told me not to—"

Seeing me, Susie wailed, "I don't know what to *do*, Mr. Hanson, I'm so torn up! I have to wear the ribbon. . ."

As Susie continued to speak and sob, I said to Kathy, "Go back to your office. I'll handle this." Then I got a thought, and I added, "Kathy, if you see an ambulance come on the lot, don't tell anybody what it's for." Kathy nodded, and left.

NAMES HAVE POWER 39

Susie's brain is stuck in an endless loop, and I'm responsible!

I reached my hand out to Susie, to give emotional support to her. Her free hand seized my hand, a long fingernail poking me in the process.

This started me wondering. The same Command of mine that made Susie start wearing hair ribbons also made her get inch-long fingernails. When I told her to shorten her nails, she did, without her brain locking up. What had I said that time that was different from when I talked today about the ribbon?

But then I realized, I don't have to understand how the Power worked. Since I had worked the Power on myself, I knew what to say to get what I wanted. The one time I'd gone against my some-how-knowing, I'd made this mess. The way to fix the mess was to let my Power-rewired brain and its somehow-knowing do what they wanted to do.

Well, it was good that I had a solution, because Susie was continuing in misery.

I looked at Susie, and let my mouth run. "Susan, what I *meant* to say was, 'From now on, don't wear an *ugly* ribbon.' Like a brown-plaid ribbon, or orange-and-green camouflage, that's what I meant. I said it wrong."

Susie blinked, and stopped crying. She took a shuddering breath, and looked at the ribbon in her hand. "Mr. Hanson, I—that is, I want so much for you to—I mean, I can't—is *this* ribbon okay to wear?"

"Yes, that ribbon goes well with your skirt. Now, please go to the restroom and fix your makeup, and please put the ribbon back in your hair. Then take the rest of the day off with pay."

Susie rushed up to me, threw her arms around me, and said, "You're a wonderful boss!" Smiling, she then grabbed her purse and dashed off to the ladies' room.

I felt like shit.

A minute later, I was standing in Kathy's office. I used my Power to convince Kathy that nothing weird had happened—I explained that Susie had caught a fever, which I sent her home because of. "And by the way, Kathy, please don't talk about this to anyone else at the dealership. Susan would appreciate that."

After dealing with Susie and Kathy, I needed to decompress. I was thirsty anyway, so when I headed to the breakroom to buy a soda, I stayed there to drink it.

Employees, for some reason, don't linger in the breakroom when the boss sits there. After five minutes, I was alone—except for the TV in the corner. On TV was Jack Wilson. At Dad's funeral, Jack's "condolences" I'd ranked in the Top Three for *in*sincerity.

Right now, Jack was doing a commercial for his own dealership; and even with the TV sound turned low, I could hear every word. Jack was talking as loudly and excitedly as if he'd just won the lottery—but instead, he was talking about this week's quote-unquote "sale"—

"And this weekend, our *already* low, low prices will be even *lower*! You *gotta* come down and check us out!"

Sheesh, give me a break, I thought.

I'd been a car dealer for less than a week, and already I loved it. The money was good, but that was only part of the thrill.

To walk through an inventory lot of hundreds of cars, and they all look great and smell new, and every car has my name on it—that's a delight. To be there and watch when a young man comes on the lot looking for a used car, because he thinks that a *used* car is all he can afford, and we put him into the first new car he's ever owned, so his kids get as excited as Christmas morning and the guy's wife thinks he's a hero—then *I* feel like a hero too.

But I really dreaded making years and years of stupid car commercials, which was my duty to my dealership. C'mon, everybody old enough to sign a legal contract is old enough to know that Tim Hanson Ford's salespeople work on commission—if we shaft the customer, we make more money; if we sell cheap, the salesman starves. So why insult the customer by talking about "low prices" that can never be low? For that matter, why call something a "sale" that happens once a week, or once a month? Jeez, no wonder the public distrusts car salesmen!

I crushed the soda can between my hands, threw it in the Recycle box, and stood up. As I headed for the door, I turned my mind to the more immediate problem of naming a general sales manager to replace Mike.

Chapter 8
Owning A Sex Slave

It was a few hours after I'd sent Susie home for her "fever," when I remembered that Deborah was scheduled to work tonight. I stepped out of the showroom and phoned Deborah's cel.

"Good afternoon, Master! This slave wishes to serve."

"First things first: Don't lose my house key, Deborah. I might not hear the doorbell at two in the morning."

"This slave will keep careful track of your key, Master. This slave is honored to be trusted with a key to your house. Does Master require anything else?"

"Actually, what you keep saying is what I'm calling about. Deborah, when you talk to anyone but me, I command you to say 'I' or 'me' instead of 'Deborah' or 'this slave'—and I command you to refer to me in public as 'Tim,' not 'Master.' If you talk to me where someone might overhear you, say 'I' and 'me' and 'Tim,' but not the word 'obey.' "

"This slave obeys, Master."

"Great! And if I'd phoned you at the club, what would you say instead of 'this slave obeys, Master'?"

"I'd say, uh, 'I will, Tim.' "

"Great, you understand. One more thing, and this is very important, Deborah: Do not do anything illegal. Avoid everything that's drug-related, don't solicit the customers, and don't whore with the customers."

"Do you know that this slave would not say no if you pimped this slave?"

"Not going there, Deborah. You owe me money, and you'll pay it off, but this whole deal bothers my conscience enough as it is."

"You are wonderful, Master. This slave loves you."

Because I choose not to pimp you? My Power does weird shit sometimes.

Later, sometime between midnight and dawn, I awoke to a line of bright light coming from the bathroom, and the sound of sink faucets spraying. Shading my eyes with my hand, I croaked, "Deborah?"

The faucet sounds stopped, and Deborah stepped into my bedroom. "Oh, Master, this slave didn't mean to wake you!"

"It's okay. How'd you do tonight?"

Deborah grabbed her purse that had been hanging from the doorknob, opened her purse, and pulled out a wad of cash. "Master, this slave earned you $217 tonight. And that's without this slave doing anything illegal, although"—her smile was proud and sexy—"this slave got two *offers*." Deborah kicked her shoes off and sashayed toward my bed, dropping the green bills like rose petals as she moved closer.

"Deb, I'm glad you did well, but I need to go back to sleep."

"Oh! Sorry, Master. But don't worry, this slave knows how to zonk you out."

She did, too—after roughly a half-hour, I fell asleep and stayed asleep (till the alarm went off). But her method was a little different: It didn't require sleeping pills, but it *did* require nudity (hers and mine), and encouraged a condom. And during that half-hour that Deborah gave me her sleep therapy, I was *very* wide awake!

The next morning, while Deborah was cooking eggs, I opened up a brand-new notebook to its first page. I picked up a pen and wrote, "CREDIT: $217.00; BALANCE: $217.00."

"What is that, Master?" Deborah asked. "Something for the dealership?"

"Actually, it's for you," I said. "I'm writing down the money you pay me, as a credit. I'm charging you half the cost of groceries, as a debit. If you have to pay income tax beyond withholding, that'll be a debit too. I'm not charging you for rent or utilities. When your balance reaches forty-three thousand, I'll free you. Feel free to check this notebook for yourself, anytime you wish."

"Oh." From her tone, she didn't know what to make of all this. Finally she said, "Anytime you wish to free this slave is okay with this slave, Master."

"Well, Deborah won't feel that way, once she's freed. And Deborah should know that she wasn't kept one day longer than necessary, or worked for one more dollar than necessary."

Even so, Deborah probably will use a meat cleaver on me in the first minute of her freedom, I thought. *She volunteered only for her body to be enslaved, not her mind.*

Chapter 9
A Date With Platinuma

Monday at six p.m., I was sitting at a table in a Chinese restaurant, waiting for Sarah/Platinuma to show up for our date. Minutes passed, and still no Sarah.

And then she was just inside the front door, looking for me. I waved, and she walked toward my table, with a smile on her face.

(Actually, she didn't walk, she prowled across the carpet. Add in the sexy gaze she was giving me, and Sarah the big-breasted platinum blonde looked sexier in blue jeans and t-shirt—and stilettos—than did the hostess in her *cheongsam*.)

"Sorry I'm late, honey"—Sarah gave me a five-second kiss— "but I had to drive all roundabout, so Duke couldn't follow me. Plus I'm not used to the Smith Freeway at rush hour. Forgive me?" Sarah took a seat to my left.

I said, "I'm sorry you're worried about Duke. You still nervous about the other night, or is there a new problem with him?"

Both Sarah's face and her voice got tense. "Um, Tim honey, can we talk about Duke later? I really want to enjoy my evening." She smiled at me. "With my *new boyfriend*."

Ten minutes later, I was saying to Sarah, ". . .mother was a Car Show Cutie, who married Dad because, she's often said, 'Big Tim is the real deal.' "

Sarah was smiling. "That's so sweet."

I continued, "Meanwhile, what Dad used to say was, 'I'm married to the nicest woman in the world, *and* the most beautiful woman in the world. I should be arrested for bigamy!' "

She laughed. "Your family sounds so happy." I felt a hand on my knee.

When Sarah and I got up to leave the restaurant, I had a raging boner. That was mainly due to Sarah rubbing my dick through my pants, through most of the meal.

As we were moving between the tables, I heard a woman's voice say, "That's Tim Hanson! You know, from commercials?"

A man's voice replied, "So that's why a hot babe like her is with a guy like that. Because he's rich."

You're not even close, pal.

Outside the restaurant, I pulled Sarah in for a kiss. She put her left arm around my neck, while her right hand was Rubbing me again. In a husky voice she said, "I think we can skip rounding the bases, and go straight to home plate."

I smiled at her. "Okay, follow me in your car to my—"

Oh shit. Slave Deborah!

I grabbed Sarah's shoulders and looked into her eyes. "Honey, I want you to spend the night with me. But you need to know: There's someone living with me for a while, and she'll be coming home about two o'clock."

Sarah shrugged. "Is she your wife? Because—"

"No, not my wife. But she—"

"Will you tell me to go home as soon as she walks in?"

"No way. But she—oh hell, Deborah's a sex slave."

I don't expect a stripper to be a hardline feminist. But when I told Sarah I was keeping a sex slave, I expected *some* kind of nasty reaction. I sure didn't expect to see Sarah *smile*.

"Mmm, my Timmy is a *love machine*. I guess I'll need to try *harder* to make you happy." Sarah's right hand began rubbing my bulge again.

Thank you, Power. Things could have gotten very ugly when I had two gorgeous women in my bedroom at the same time.

I walked Sarah to her car, then I started toward my own car. As I walked past the back of Sarah's car, I noticed that her back windshield was covered with duct tape and a big rectangle of cardboard.

I walked back to Sarah's car door and knocked on her window. Seconds later, I asked her, "What happened back there?"

She sighed. "Duke happened. He used a brick. Sometime last night, while I was working."

Fifteen minutes later, Sarah and I were in my living room, kissing. Correction: I was kissing Sarah while I rubbed her tits through her bra; Sarah, as she kissed me, was loosening my belt and unzipping me.

I grabbed my pants before they fell down around my knees, and pulled my cel phone out of my pocket. "Hold on, I need to text my slave," I said.

Sarah then grabbed the waist of my pants, dragged me to the couch, yanked my pants down, and pushed me onto the couch. "Okay, Tim honey, you text her—*if you can.*"

While I tried texting Deborah, Sarah started sucking my cock. *Eventually* I got the message sent, but before then, her blowjob made me lose concentration a lot. I'm sure the same thing has happened to you.

Chapter 10
I Put My Babes To Work

I was being shaken awake.

I looked at the bedside clock; it said 2:26. In the darkness, I heard Slave Deborah whisper: "Master, is Sarah still here? Where should this slave sleep?"

I was still nine-tenths asleep. I murmured, "Mmm, that's a good question."

I felt Sarah stir, and then she asked in a sleepy voice, "Baby, is your slave girl here?"

"Uh, yeah." I thought, *Will I need to call the cops soon?*

"Can you turn the light on, please? I've met only one sex slave before."

I thought, *"Only one" sex slave?* I turned on the table light.

"Wow, you're beautiful," each woman said at the same time.

It turned out that they knew each other, a little. Sarah and Deborah had met at another dancer's birthday party.

Then both women got silent, and I realized that each was waiting for me to make a decision. I moved to the middle of the bed and said, "Slave Deborah, get naked and get in bed with us. But no sex tonight—I'm too tired."

"Mmm, did I wear Baby out?" Sarah said. She kissed me on the cheek. To Deborah she said, "Let's hope he doesn't snore."

"He snores," Deborah said as she slid into bed and put an arm on my chest, "but it's a cute snore."

"Deborah, turn out the light and let's all sleep," I ordered.

"Yes, um. . ."

"Sarah knows about us, Slave Deborah. It's okay to use the words around her."

"Then this slave obeys, Master." Deborah turned out the light. I kissed Sarah goodnight, then Deborah goodnight, then I fell asleep.

I woke up later, when there was just enough light in the room to see shapes. Sarah and Deborah were talking quietly over my rib cage, and someone was stroking my cock.

"That feels good," I said, then I fell back asleep.

When I woke up again, Sarah was gone from the bed, and Deborah was pressed against me with her arm around my waist. My first thought was, *Is Sarah mad at me? Why is she gone?*

I tried to sit up, and that woke Deborah up. I said, "Where is Sarah?"

Deborah said, "Relax, Master, she's making breakfast in the kitchen."

"Oh, okay."

"Um, she asked this slave to let her know when you're awake."

I agreed to that, I got a "This slave obeys" in reply, and Deborah got out of bed. Then my sex slave, wearing not a stitch of clothing, sashayed off to talk to my girlfriend.

Life is good sometimes.

When Deborah walked back in the bedroom, she giggled. "She told this slave, 'Have *fun*.' "

I glanced at the clock; I had half an hour before my alarm went off. Then my arm reached out for Deborah. "I'll see that you have *lots* of fun."

I was fucking Deborah when I felt a third hand stroke my back. There by the bed stood Sarah, with a spatula in her hand and a sexy smile on her face. "Breakfast is ready," Sarah said, "*when* you two are ready."

I pulled into my parking place at the dealership only fifteen minutes late. But I'd had only five hours of sleep, and now I was feeling it.

I started the Morning Meeting by saying, "I'd like to announce that I'm promoting Betty Jane to General Manager." As everyone was applauding, I tried not to yawn.

I hadn't even finished the Morning Meeting when I realized I needed more coffee. I raised my hand in a "hold on" gesture, grabbed my empty cup, stood up—

—and Susan (who was once again dressed like a sex-fantasy secretary) jumped up as well. "Do you need more coffee? Stay there, I'll get it," she said cheerfully. "No cream, two sugars, coming right up."

I handed her the cup, and she minced off on high heels to the urn. I sat down.

"What's with Susan being so nice to you?" Kathy asked me.

"I have no idea," I said.

Kathy's face said she didn't believe me.

Betty Jane also was eyeing me. "So you and Susan aren't. . .?"

Albert said, "Ease up, you two. If the boss is tired this morning, it's not because of *her*, it's because of Gothika."

I said, "Haven't gone out with Gothika yet. Yesterday it was Platinuma."

Susan set my coffee cup down by my left hand. "Gothika, Platinuma, who are they?"

"Dancers," I said.

"At the club that Mike took him to," Albert said. "Total-babe strippers, and our new boss got both their phone numbers."

Susan said as she sat down, "And no, Betty Jane, Mr. Hanson and I *aren't* dating. But it wouldn't be sexual harassment if we *did*." She smiled at me. "But it sounds like I'd need to take a number."

After the Morning Meeting, I had a long G-rated meeting in my office with Betty Jane, as I discussed her new duties with her. As soon as Betty Jane left, I had an XXX-rated meeting in my office with Susan. This time it took Susan longer to suck me off, because my dick was sore, but Susan never complained. While Susan was slurping me, I managed to write an online help-wanted ad for Betty Jane's vacated position of Finance Manager.

After Susan left, I sat at my desk to work on paperwork—and soon discovered I'd fallen asleep in my chair. To wake myself up and get my blood pumping, I decided to walk around my dealership.

I walked into every department and let my employees know that Betty Jane was now the number-two boss and that they were to treat her with respect. With that task done, I headed for the employee breakroom, for another cup of alleged coffee.

I was sipping coffee and chewing on a chocolate bar when Bernie O'Toole's car-dealer ad come on the TV. I watched him spout off, rolled my eyes, and thought, *Jeez, why can't you simply tell the truth?*

And then I got a *great* idea. I threw the rest of the vile black liquid down my throat, and rushed back to my office.

Actually, to Susan's desk outside my office. "Susan Cooper," I said, "I am going to be making a new kind of commercial soon, and it would be *very helpful* to me if you would star in it."

Somehow I knew how she'd answer.

I called Sarah on her cel, and explained my idea. She was game. (Ain't love grand?) Deborah, I knew, had gone back to sleep, so I left a message on her cel, ordering her to be at the dealership in the morning. Next, I called the camera crew who regularly filmed Tim Hanson Ford's commercials, and gave them the where and when. With all that done, I went to talk to Hank.

If you the customer tell me that you'll buy my *new* car if I'll buy your ratty *old* car, what am I going to do? I'm not stupid, I'll take your old car in trade. But new-car dealerships have standards about what cars we'll sell on our used-car lots: late model, low mileage, mechanically sound, with nothing more than minor body damage. So what happens to the rustbuckets that we buy but won't sell? We sell those, a bunch at a time, to used-car wholesalers, who sell them to mom-and-pop used-car lots.

The point is, even the classiest car dealership has a few eyesores on the property somewhere, if you look hard enough.

Which is why I walked up to Hank, the Used-Car Sales Manager, and said, "Show me the ugliest car I own."

The next morning, Susan walked into the Morning Meeting, dressed just like she'd dressed in olden days—if you ignored the top three buttons of her blouse being unbuttoned.

"I like that you've returned to a more *professional* look, Susan," Betty Jane said.

Kathy nodded. "As opposed to looking like a—like a. . ."

Susan said brightly, "Oh, I'm only dressed like this because Mr. Hanson asked me to. For the commercial. Tomorrow, I'll be dressed in my regular clothes again."

"Commercial?" Bobby said. "Susan, you're going to be in one of our commercials?"

By now, everyone was present, so I said, "People, I'm making a major change to how we operate, and our new advertising will reflect that."

"What's the change?" Albert asked.

"It's a radical new idea, unheard-of in the car business," I said. "We're going to be honest."

Everyone but Susan stared at me.

" 'Honest'? We're honest now, we don't need to change," Kathy said.

I replied, "We're honest for car dealers. We don't roll odometers back, or put motorcycle oil into bad car engines to make them sound better. *But* I myself have sold twenty-eight cars, and I've understudied the job of every one of you, and I know there are *many* tricks to squeeze a few extra bucks out of a customer. Starting today, those tricks stop."

"You sure that's smart, Tim?" Bobby asked. "That's going to hurt your bottom line."

"It's going to hurt you too, don't think I don't know that. Short term, every one of you will see your performance-bonus drop. You might well be tempted to quit and go elsewhere. Please don't."

Susan smiled at everyone. "You said 'short term,' Mr. Hanson. You think things will get better, real quick?"

"Yes. It's a gamble, I admit that. But I think that once the public becomes convinced that we keep all promises we make, and make no promises we can't keep, that we'll be swamped."

Silence.

I added, "Which reminds me. Starting today, this minute, our people are *forbidden* to use the words 'lowest price' and 'highest price.' As in, 'We will sell you a Ford for the lowest price in town, and give you the highest value for your trade.' If a salesman wouldn't say something to his grandmother, the salesman better not say it to anyone else. Or I'll have his ass."

Fifteen minutes later, the Morning Meeting ended, and my managers walked out of my office (while giving each other "the boss is an idiot" looks). Waiting outside by Susan's desk were the camera crew, as well as Sarah and Deborah.

Susan handed out copies of the contracts (which Sarah and Deborah signed), Susan handed out copies of the script, then we left to shoot the commercial.

A young office worker (SUSAN) is standing
by the open hood of an old car. BLACK SMOKE
RISES FROM THE ENGINE. Susan has a black

oil smudge on each of her cheeks and her forehead. Susan looks sad.

A red late-model Mustang convertible drives by, with two young women in it. SARAH is driving the Mustang; DEBORAH is riding shotgun.

DEBORAH (to Sarah): We need to help her!

CUT TO:
The red Mustang is parked on the shoulder, ahead of the dead old car. On the back of the Mustang, instead of a regular license plate, is a "Tim Hanson Ford" dealer tag. Sarah and Deborah are peering into the old car's engine compartment as Susan gestures.

(Note that while nobody is dressed slutty or sexy, it is clear at a glance that these are three very attractive young women.)

SARAH: You need a new car.

SUSAN: I don't know anything about cars. I'm afraid a dealer will cheat me.

DEBORAH: Then you should go to Tim Hanson Ford. They've started a No Cheat Guarantee.

SUSAN: They work on commission, right? They'll make more money if they cheat me.

SARAH: True, but the new owner, Timothy Richard Hanson, wants you to come back in five years. And ten years. And twenty

years. And he wants you to tell your
friends and coworkers to go to Tim Hanson
Ford. He knows you won't do that if you
think he's picked your pocket.

SUSAN: And if I <u>do</u> get cheated there, <u>then</u>
what?

DEBORAH: Then Tim Hanson <u>fires</u> the guy!
Right then!

SUSAN: Tim Hanson Ford is on Smith Freeway,
right?

SARAH: Yes. Tim Hanson Ford is on Smith
Freeway northbound, a quarter-mile north of
the Woodrow Wilson exit.

Chapter 11
The Commercial Airs

The next week was crazy at Tim Hanson Ford.

The commercial aired during the noontime news of three TV stations, roughly twenty-four hours after we'd started shooting it. Our phone started ringing. Half the callers asked, "Your 'No Cheat Guarantee,' you don't really mean that, do you?" The other half of our callers demanded to know, "Who are those *babes*?"

By six that evening, the ad was posted on YouTube, and I was getting calls from "The Today Show" and "Good Morning America." The next morning I had to pass up a blowjob from Deborah because I was doing "live via satellite" TV interviews.

Two days later, a customer came to my office and told me that he'd overheard Jeff (a salesman I'd never liked) tell a young couple that he was overestimating their income on the loan application "so that you'll be sure to be approved." Reputable car salesmen disapprove of such a practice; it sticks the car-buyer with payments he can't afford. The dishonest car salesman has long since spent his commission check when the repo truck hauls the overextended borrower's car away.

With the snitching customer tagging along, I confronted Jeff McBeal, who admitted his misdeed to me. (Amazing, huh?) The customer's jaw dropped when, just as I'd promised, I fired Jeff then and there.

What I didn't know until next morning was that the customer who'd tattled on Jeff was a local newspaper reporter, doing an undercover investigation. The newspaper article not only described the Jeff situation, but also outed Susan as the damsel-in-distress in the commercial. The article's headline was "Wow, Tim Hanson means it."

Chapter 12
Dinner With Gothika

On the phone I heard Susan's voice. "Mr. Hanson, you have a call from a Jeanette McAllister. She says it's . . . *personal?*" Susan's voice sounded puzzled.

I was puzzled too; I didn't recognize the name. "Hello, this is Tim Hanson."

"Mister Hanson, I am Slave Jeanette, and Mistress Gothika—"

"Oh, you mean Ashley?"

"Mistress will be pleased that you remembered her name. Anyway, Mistress *Ashley* has commanded that I invite you to dinner with us, either tomorrow night or the night after, whichever is convenient for you."

"That's short notice. Do you know why she said *those* nights, and not later?"

"Mistress did not confide her reasons to her slave. But I know that she's off, those nights."

And Sarah works both those nights. Could supposedly lesbian Ashley be making a play for me? I wondered. Aloud I said, "Tomorrow night's fine. I can be there at six-thirty."

The following evening at 6:30, I was holding a bottle of wine as I stood at Ashley's front door, in a prosperous part of town. I rang the doorbell.

When strawberry-blond Jeanette opened the door, I recognized her as a dancer at the Nimfo Club. Now she was dressed in white platform stilettos, a white micro-miniskirt, and a white fishnet "blouse" that did nothing to cover her unbrassiered tits. Jeanette gave me a spokesmodel smile and said, "Mistress welcomes you and invites you to enter."

"Freely and of your own will," added a woman's voice from behind Jeanette.

I walked through the door and past Jeanette. Ashley/Gothika stood there in a black-leather dress that was cut like an evening gown with slits up the side. Needless to say, the dress flattered Ashley's gigantic tits. Her hair and fingernails were still black, her lipstick was midnight red, her eye shadow was midnight purple, and she was wearing black-skull dangling earrings.

She smiled at me and said, "Thank you for bringing wine. Slave Jeanette, kiss Tim on the cheek and then pour three glasses of wine. You may take an equal share."

"Yes, Mistress." Jeanette obediently kissed my cheek, and then took the wine bottle into the kitchen.

Ashley laughed. "Fuck, Tim, it is *such* a relief that you have a slave of your own! There's so much explanation I can skip. Did your girl really become your slave to save her Corvette?"

I shrugged. "That, and to stay out of jail."

By now, Ashley had led me to facing overstuffed chairs. Jeanette walked up, handed Ashley and me each a wineglass, then sat on the right arm of Ashley's chair. Ashley reached over and moved her right hand inside Jeanette's tiny skirt, while Ashley sipped the wine that she held in her left hand. No panties covered Jeanette's shaved pussy. If Jeanette was embarrassed at being masturbated in front of me, she didn't say so.

Less than a minute later, Jeanette bit her lip. "I'm close to cumming, Mistress."

Ashley withdrew her hand, wiping her wet fingers on Jeanette's skirt. "Serve dinner now, slave. Make me be pleased with you. You may pull your skirt down."

Jeanette glanced at me, then said, "Thank you, Mistress." She stood up, tugged on her skirt, and walked into the kitchen. Jeanette's face was red, her nipples jutted out, and she smelled like hot pussy.

During dinner, I explained how Deborah had become my slave. (Except that I didn't mention my Power's part in Deborah's enslavement.) Then I asked, "So Jeanette, tell me, how did it happen with you?"

Jeanette said, "It started in high school. We both were going to the same high school—"

"Slave, why are you speaking with a man without my permission?" Ashley asked, with bite in her voice.

"But Mistress, he told me to tell him—"

I realized what the problem was: my Power had made Jeanette answer my question. So it was up to me to fix things. Something I said must've worked, because seconds later, Ashley was smiling across the table. "Slave Jen-Jen, you are forgiven." Ashley made a gesture toward Jeanette, *Continue your story.*

Jeanette said, "We both were in Grand City Central High. I was a cheerleader in the Junior class. Ashley was a Senior and a Goth."

I laughed. "Why am I not surprised?"

"Anyway, Ashley saw a mouse in the school cafeteria, so she organized a cafeteria boycott. I'd blown her off before—she wasn't cool, she wasn't popular—but with this boycott, she took charge. She was *strong*. She was a *goddess*."

"Did it work?" I asked Ashley. "The boycott?"

"Yeah, eventually, after I went around to all the cliques—jocks and cheerleaders, stoners, nerds—and made my case. Several times. At first the school said, 'We don't have the budget for an extra exterminator visit,' but a week later, they caved."

I turned to the strawberry blonde. "So Jeanette, how did you two hook up?"

Jeanette made eye contact with Ashley, then said, "On the second day of the boycott, I started keeping her company outside the cafeteria during lunch hour. And on one of those days—"

"Fourth day of the boycott," Ashley said, "which was your third lunchtime to be hanging with me."

"Anyway, lunch hour was almost over and she said, 'Fuck, I forgot to get my Shakespeare book. Jeanette, go fetch it out of my locker and bring it here before the bell rings.' So I did."

I nodded. "She didn't ask you to, she ordered you to."

Jeanette said, "And that's how my slavery to Mistress started."

Ashley said, "As soon as she handed me the book, I kissed her, right in the school hallway. The hallway was *empty*, but still! When I kissed her and she didn't freak, I knew I had her." Ashley smiled, then said, "And now she's my stripper sex slave."

A few minutes later, Ashley said to me, "In your commercial, Sarah was driving the Mustang, and another dancer was in the passenger seat—"

I nodded. "My slave Deborah."

Ashley said, "So the women in the Mustang were dancers I know. But who was the third dancer?"

I said blankly, "Third dancer?"

"The blond hottie whose old clunker broke down. Where does *she* work at?"

"She's not a stripper. She's my receptionist."

"Oh, *really*," Ashley said, her voice dropping an octave. "Well, if she decides to earn extra cash as a dancer, I'll be glad to help in *any* way I can."

"I'll tell her, if Susie mentions anything. But I don't think she's interested."

A few minutes later, Ashley asked, "So are you going to make more of those commercials? With the three women?"

I said, "Sure. These ads are different than what the other dealers are doing."

"They certainly are," Ashley said, laughing. Then her eyes went a little out of focus, as if she was thinking hard about something.

Dinner was over, and we all three walked into the living room. I sat down on the couch, but then Ashley walked over to me, knelt in front of me, and smiled at me. I got a magnificent view of magnificent tits.

"Tim," she said, "I've *really* enjoyed having you as my guest. You're interesting to talk with." Fifteen seconds later, her mouth was on my cock.

She sucked me fast. She sucked me slow. Her tongue swirled my head. She tongued my wrinkled spot. She deepthroated me. I was reminded again that she had been able to pay cash for a new car by charging big money for her blowjobs, and she was giving me this one for free.

Actually, she gave me 1-1/2 blowjobs for free. She sucked me to orgasm (which felt glorious), then milked me to limpness, then kept sucking me till I was hard and happy again.

Ashley pulled her mouth off my erect cock, then stood up. "Slave Jeanette, take Tim into the guest bedroom and fuck him till I tell you to stop. You have permission to cum."

"Thank you, Mistress," Jeanette said, as she eyed my cock. Her nipples were hard.

Jeanette took me into a small room that was nearly filled by a double bed. As soon as I shut the door, Jeanette started to undress.

"What are you doing?" I asked.

"I'm undressing," she said. Seeing my puzzled look, she added, "I get naked, then I undress you, then you have me."

"Stop, Jeanette. Stop right there. Let *me* undress you."

It didn't take long, because she wasn't wearing much. And I swear, she was getting off on it. I said to her, "Jeanette, tell me why this excites you."

She was flushed now. "Because it's been so long since anyone undressed me."

"And that doesn't bother you?"

Jeanette shrugged. "Now it's my turn to do you."

She did a lot of stroking and caressing in the process of undressing me—more than was necessary to remove my clothing. All that touching of Jeanette's was making my cock twitch. She had just pulled my shorts to the floor, and I was just stepping out of them, when the bedroom door opened.

I turned around to see Ashley leaning against the doorjamb, leering at us. She said, "Goody, I'm just in time for the fireworks."

I said, "Ahem. People get privacy for what Jeanette and I are about to do."

"You're in my house. You're about to fuck my slave. I'm entitled to see this," Ashley replied.

I sighed. "I remind you that I'm not a rutting stud bull, and I'm not another of your slaves—I don't have to play your game. Ashley, you have two choices: You walk out now, and shut the door and wait till we're done, *or* you get naked now and I fuck you too."

"I don't like *either* of those choices."

"Otherwise, I get dressed right now and I leave, leaving Jeanette horny and needy. And Ashley, you care for Jeanette too much to let her suffer so."

Ashley's face, which had been looking at me with a challenging and stubborn expression, now softened as she looked at Jeanette lying on the bed. Ashley said, "It's true, I care for Jeanette very much." Turning to face me again, Ashley said, "Enjoy yourselves." She shut the door as she walked out.

Jeanette looked at me in shock. "How did you *do* that? Mistress *never* gives in when she argues with a man!"

I shrugged. "Right now, I'm more concerned about the fact that I'm in bed with a healthy young woman, and she's horny. I can't let this continue."

Now, I exercise, I'd like to think I'm charming, and it looks like I'm not going to lose my hair. Still, when I reached my hand down between her legs, I wasn't ready for how *wet* Jeanette was.

"Oh god, please fuck me!" she begged.

I kissed her face. She was a good kisser. While I continued to feel up her pussy (and she writhed and moaned), I moved myself down her body to suck on her nipples. She gasped when my mouth first made contact there.

After a while, I started to move down lower, intending to eat her out, when she said, "*Later!* Right now I want your meaty male cock in me!"

I obliged her. As soon as I put my cock in her, she wrapped her legs around me and cried, "Oh god!"

She was wet and eager and vocal. She scratched my back and she thrust her hips. She moaned, she grunted, and she screamed. And did I mention, she was wet?

By the time I spurted, Jeanette had come four times that I was sure of. As I was thrusting and gasping, she grabbed my head and kissed me like a leech. "Oh, I can feel you come in me, I made you feel good, you made me feel good. Tim, you are such a real man, you're my man-lover." All the time she was talking, she kept trying to also kiss me.

Eventually I rolled off her and onto the bed. Jeanette pushed my shoulder to roll me onto my back. "I have to clean your cock," she said with a smile.

She cleaned my cock with her lips and tongue. She did such a thorough job cleaning my cock, fifteen minutes after she started, I was spurting again. Unlike Ashley, Jeanette didn't deepthroat me, but she did swallow me, so I was happy.

I really don't enjoy eating out a pussy that I've recently come in. I *really* don't. But I'd promised Jeanette a pussy-licking, so I manned up and ate her out. I figured she'd be used to such a thing and get bored, but she screamed and thrashed when I licked her clit.

Minutes later, Jeanette and I were getting dressed. She had been wearing a lot less than me, and so finished first. When I was dressed and ready to leave the bedroom, I found her kneeling on the floor, her heels pressing the door shut.

She looked at me and said quietly, "If you tell me to come with you when you leave, I will. I will be your slave from now on, if you command me so."

"But you are Ashley's slave."

"But you bested her when you two argued tonight. You dominated her. You deserve to claim me."

I said, "You mean all this as a compliment to me, so thank you. But Deborah's boyfriend stole from my father, so I wasn't willing to forgive the debt, and that's the *only* reason I have a slave. Jeanette, believe me, I don't wake up each morning wishing that I had more slaves."

She sighed. "Which is one of the things that makes you a good master." She stood up and kissed me on the lips. Then she turned away and opened the bedroom door.

Ashley, with Jeanette trailing behind, walked me to the front door. Ashley put her hand on my arm, the only time she had touched me all evening (if you didn't count digging my cock out of my pants to blow me). Ashley said, "I ask you to put me in your next commercial."

"I'll see," I replied.

I shook Ashley's hand, then glanced past her to Jeanette, who was watching me closely. "Goodnight, you two," I said, and left.

Chapter 13
Gothika's Offer

It was almost lunchtime the next day when my phone rang. Susan said, "Mister Hansen, there are two women here to see you. They say it's personal." Lowering her voice, Susan added, "One of them is Jeanette McAllister. I recognize her voice."

I asked, "Does the other woman have black hair and humongous breasts?"

"Yes and *definitely* yes," Susan said. Then she again lowered her voice and added, "And she's looking at me like I'm a box of chocolates. She's already asked if I have a boyfriend."

"Susan, for sure I'd love to hear the answer to that myself."

"I *had* a boyfriend. His name was Adlai. I dated him because he supported my freeing myself from the shackles of male oppression. But the other day, when I was getting my hair dyed blond? I realized then, men like Adlai didn't interest me anymore. He's *too* liberated, you know? So that night, I broke up with him."

Very interesting, I thought. But aloud I said, "Susan, go ahead and send Ashley and Jeanette into my office."

Seconds later, the two strippers walked through the door. Jeanette was dressed in pea-green clothing that was conservative. Well, as conservative as a woman with long strawberry-blond hair, breast implants, an athletic figure, and a pretty face could manage.

On the other hand, Ashley didn't bother trying to look sedate—*her* outfit was black skyscraper heels under a three-piece outfit of black pinstripe wool that showed a lot of tit. (Perhaps because Ashley *has* a lot of tit.) My guess was, her ensemble was part of Frederick's of Hollywood's Don Corleone Collection.

"Me and Jeanette, we have a problem," Ashley said. "With you."

Without being invited to, Ashley walked to the chair facing my desk and sat down. Jeanette moved to stand next to her, her hand on Ashley's shoulder.

"Tell me the problem, Ashley," I said.

Ashley glanced up at Jeanette. "Slave Jeanette is hot for you. Beyond her sometimes getting the urge for cock, I mean. *You*, she's super-hot for. And last night, I realized I want Jen-Jen to be happy, and it bugs me when she's not."

"I see. And Jeanette, what do *you* have to say about what she said?"

"I can't stop thinking about you fucking me," Jeanette replied. "I fantasize about me fucking you not because *she* orders me to, but because *you* order me to. And maybe I'm in love with you."

Ashley's head whipped around. "You didn't tell me that."

I said, "I'm flattered, ladies, I really am. But I don't understand, why is this a crisis? C'mon, surely Jeanette has had crushes on guys before."

"Not really," Jeanette said, "not since I hooked up with Ashley. Guys are all immature, wimpy, or bullshitters, truly. But you're the real deal."

"You're not interested in guys you meet at Nimfo Club?" I asked.

Both women laughed. Ashley said, "Guys who come to strip clubs are losers!"

"Really, Ashley? You met *me* at your strip club."

"Because Mike dragged you there. If you'd walked in our door under your own steam, we wouldn't be having this conversation."

"So why are you two here, Ashley? What do you want from me?"

The mobster-wannabee stripper answered with a strange question: "How many bedrooms are in your house?"

"Two or three," I said, my face showing my puzzlement. "I have three bedrooms, but I use one as a home office, and I'd put a bed in there only in an emergency. Why?"

"Jen-Jen wants to serve you, but also wants to serve me; and I want Jen-Jen to be happy. So here's my idea: I move my queen-sized bed into an empty bedroom of your house, and Jeanette moves her twin bed into your bedroom or wherever it'll fit. Then you fuck her whenever you want."

"I'm sorry, but—"

"You haven't heard the sweetener."

"Go."

"I pay you five hundred bucks a month, and I myself give you two blowjobs a week."

"Ashley, I like you, but right now you're a stripper *and a whore*. Being a whore means your phone ringing all the time, and you coming and going a lot. Denied."

"What about a thousand bucks a month, three blowjobs a week, and I quit the hooking?"

Now it was Jeanette's head that whipped around. "You'd really stop?"

Ashley replied, "Why not? House is nearly paid for, and it's a bitch dodging vice-squad cops." To me, Ashley said, "You still don't get to fuck *me*, but I figure you'll survive. Oh yeah, three sucks a week from me, plus Sarah and two slave girls fucking and sucking you whenever you want? You'll survive."

Not to mention, a blowjob every morning from Susan, I thought.

"Do we have a deal?" Jeanette pressed.

I picked up my phone. "As soon as I bounce it off Sarah, *maybe* we have a deal."

I expected Sarah to blow a gasket—or at least to pout and cry. Instead, she said, "My Tim the Honey Dick is becoming a real stud muffin. Just save some for me, sweetie, okay?"

I hung up the phone and told my visitors, "I'll be home around six. You guys can bring stuff then."

I walked my visitors out to Ashley's pink Lexus, then returned to my office. Susan stopped her transparent attempt at looking busy as soon as I passed by her desk. She asked me, "Can I ask what that was about?"

I shrugged. "Tonight I'll have two more women moving into my house."

"Two *more* women?" Susan repeated, her eyebrows shooting up.

"Uh, yeah," I said, kicking myself. I hadn't told Susan about my unusual home life, lest she blast me with a feminist rant.

But instead, Susan smiled and nodded. "So long as they're not working for you, good for you."

"Actually, they are. Remember the other girls in the commercial? But Sarah and Deborah moved in with me before then."

Susan lightly punched my arm and grinned at me. "Sounds like you're getting that harem you've always wanted."

Realizing that Susan was right, I started getting erect. Which Susan immediately noticed. "Oh, my poor boss," she said. "I wouldn't be helpful if I left you distracted by a hard-on."

So saying, she took me by the hand, dragged me into my office, shut the door, and dropped to her knees. I got my second Susan-blowjob of the day.

It's good to be king.

Chapter 14
Ashley + Ashley + Ashley

That Monday, I announced at the end of the Morning Meeting that I was taking the rest of the day off—my first day off since my father's heart attack. Susie offered to walk me to my car.

"You'll never guess what I did this weekend," she told me.

"I give up."

"I moved into a new apartment. Meadow Green Apartments, number 262. Have you heard of them? They're in the 119-hundred block of Grant Drive."

"I know them, they're, uh, near the dealership." *They're also less than five—*

Susie clapped her hands. "*And* my new apartment is three minutes from your house! I checked last night. So feel free to drop in anytime, for coffee or . . . whatever."

"Wouldn't that be inappropriate behavior?"

She slapped my arm. "*No,* silly, not unless I move into *your house.* But if you come to my apartment, I can give you a hot, wet fuck anytime you want. That's just acting friendly."

"To put it mildly," I said.

By now we were at my car. Which was parked next to Susie's car. Through the window glass of Susie's car, I could see a small cardboard box on the passenger seat. The box was filled with hardback and paperback books.

"What's with the books?" I asked.

She blushed. "I'm going to donate them to Salvation Army after work."

"What have you got?"

She blushed redder. "Nothing you'd want to read. They're books I've outgrown."

I put up my hands. "Sorry, didn't mean to pry. But I'm curious, and your acting mysterious isn't helping it."

Without planning to, I'd said the magic words. Susie pressed the button on her door-lock remote. As her car doors THUNK'd, she said, "Please don't think I'm still a bitch."

Seconds later, I had her passenger door open, and I was pulling books out of the box. I remarked, "You're right. *The Politics of Virginity*, *A History of Male Oppression*, *Genetics and Gender Roles: A New Paradigm*, and *Castrating Bitches: A Manifesto*—none of these books are what I would want to read."

Susie now was blushing all the way down to her throat. "Like I said, I've outgrown them. They all seem so *shrill* now. And if feminism means that a woman is free to choose, can't I choose to dress sexy and give heart-stopping blowjobs?"

"No argument from me," I said.

Less than ten minutes later, I stepped into my house quietly, because I knew that Sarah and Slave Deborah had gone back to sleep as soon as I'd left for work.

A little after ten in the morning, my doorbell rang. It was Ashley and Slave Jeanette, ready to move stuff in.

They weren't moving a lot in, basically clothes and a bed each, so I didn't expect them to show up with a moving trailer. And they didn't—instead, they showed up in the company of two young men and a pick-up truck.

The whole time the two guys' backs and arms were working, the men wore horn-dog smiles and their eyes were ogling Ashley and Slave Jeanette. And when a yawning Slave Deborah walked out of my bedroom, wearing an oversized green t-shirt and nothing else, the movers' grins got bigger. (So did Ashley's.)

When the mover-guys' hands were free, I introduced myself, stuck out my hand, and asked them their names. Seconds later, I was asking, "So, Steven, Benjamin, tell me: What are you being paid for this?"

"We're not sure yet," Steven said. "Gothika didn't exactly *promise* anything, you know? Not specifically." He looked unworried.

Benjamin said, "But she *did* tell us that she and Peachy would be *very grateful* if we'd help them out." Benjamin's leer told me how he thought that the strippers' "gratitude" would be expressed.

"Uh-*huh*," I said. I left in search of my newest roommates. I found Ashley and Slave Jeanette in my bedroom, talking with Sarah and Slave Deborah.

"So, Ashley," I said, "what are you planning to pay Steven and Benjamin for their hard work and the use of their truck?"

Ashley smiled. "Ten bucks apiece at first, but I'll let them talk me up to twenty."

"Really? *They* think they're going to get some kind of sex from you two."

"But I didn't *promise* them that. I didn't promise them anything. If they didn't nail me down to a fixed payment before they started, that's their own fault."

"Just so I'm clear, Ashley: You don't intend to give blowjobs, tit-fucks, or pussy-fucks to these guys? Neither yourself nor Slave Jeanette paying them with sex?"

Ashley smirked. "Please! Aren't I a lesbian?"

I frowned. "Ashley Baker, I'm keenly disappointed in you. You led those guys on, using carefully chosen words and tone of voice and body language to promise those guys sex in so many words, making promises which you had no intention of keeping. Lesbian or not, what you did was vile."

A moment ago, Ashley had been smirking; now she looked ready to cry. "I am so sorry! What should I do?"

"Didn't you tell me that up till yesterday you charged seventy-five bucks?"

"For a plain-vanilla blowjob, yeah."

"Then give each guy a refund for the blowjob he doesn't get. Pay them seventy-five apiece, Ashley."

Ashley should have argued a blue streak. But thanks to my Power, she didn't argue; instead she hung her head and said, "That sounds fair."

Being the sultan of a growing harem doesn't stop my grass from growing. After Ashley and Jeanette unpacked their stuff and we five toasted the move-in with Budweisers, I went outside to mow my lawn.

I cut the side yards and back yard first, because that's the easy part—my pool means I don't have to mow as much. I had just started on the front yard when Gothika sashayed out, a glass of pink lemonade in her hand. I let the mower die.

"Hey, you *hard*-working man," she said when she got close. She reached into a pocket of her black denim miniskirt and pulled out ten hundred-dollar bills, which she handed to me. She said, "Why don't you take a break and come inside now? I'll fix you lunch. Then you can sit on the couch and"—she licked her lips—"I'll make sure you *enjoy* your meal."

I said, "Nah, it's getting hot. If I stop now, I'll be cooking my brain when I go back outside."

Ashley said, "Then how about we go into the garage, and I'll tonsil your tool by your toolbox? Eight minutes max, guaranteed. Please? I've never sucked cock in a garage before."

"Why are you so hot-to-trot to suck my cock *right now*?"

"Maybe I've suddenly realized how incredibly attractive you are, hmm?"

"Ashley, Ashley, Ashley. Don't stand in front of me and lie, not even for a joke."

"Okay, fine," she said. "After you went out to cut the grass, I tried getting service from Jen-Jen. You know, to christen my new digs? But *I couldn't enjoy it.* All I could think of was, 'I promised Tim a thousand bucks a month and three blowjobs a week, and I haven't paid up yet.' So I need to get square with you, so I can get my clit licked and enjoy it."

"Uh-*huh*," I said. "Ashley, wait till later for that first one here. I'm not interested in getting sexy with you right now."

"*Ahem!*" a man's voice said, behind me.

I turned around. Standing on the sidewalk was "Brother Simon" Effib, along with his wife and teen daughter. Brother Simon was giving me a disgusted look.

"Brother Simon" owned a nicer house than I did. He lived in a mansion that filled the cul-de-sac that was at the end of my street.

And you know how it is—some people think that if they own a bigger house than you, or a nicer car, they're a better human being than you are. I was coming to suspect that Brother Simon was one of those snobs.

Both Brother Simon's wife and his daughter were looking at me intently, which was strange.

If you've ever tuned in to one of those church broadcasts, you know what the three Effibs looked like. Brother Simon had a pompadour. His wife had bleached-blond and teased hair, well-selected but understated makeup, and well-tailored and conservatively cut (but brightly colored) clothing. The teen was dressed the same as her mother, making allowances for age, and so looked like the poster girl for corn-fed wholesome innocence.

"Mister Hanson," said Brother Simon to me, "we've noticed that several *flamboyant* women have moved into your house recently, of which *she* is typical." He pointed his chin at Gothika.

"Oh, you mean us *strippers*?" Gothika said. "Yeah, there are four of us erotic dancers living with Tim now. Is that a problem?"

" 'Is that a problem?' Woman, this is a god-fearing, tax-paying neighborhood that believes in Christian family values. We do not want immorality here. More to the point, we do not want immoral women here!"

I interrupted him with " 'We' do not? Are your wife and daughter mute?" I turned to look at them. "What say you two? Do you call four women whom you've never met, 'immoral'?"

"Because they're strippers?" the daughter said. "I honestly don't know. But if I looked like your girlfriend, I'd be tempted to find out after high school, how immoral a stripper's life could be."

"Ashley Lynn! Be quiet!" Brother Simon said.

"Just being truthful, Father. Part of me is curious to know how much men would pay to see me naked. And I'm *really* curious whether Mister Hanson would pay to see me naked."

Gothika strolled up to the girl and looked her up and down, as if Daddy wasn't mere feet away and glaring. "Girlie, you have a pretty face, and your legs are shaped nice, but you need to get 'work' done." Gothika hefted her giant tits.

"Silence, woman!" Brother Simon said. "Ashley Lynn! Home, now!"

The daughter rolled her eyes, smiled at me, then turned toward her house. As she walked away, she murmured, "Now I'll *definitely* have to wait." I had no idea what she meant by that.

Meanwhile, Brother Simon's wife was saying, "I'm torn. A big part of me does think that stripping is immoral. But I'm like Ashley Lynn—part of me wants to know that Tim Hanson and other men would pay to see me naked."

"Ashley Sue, stop saying these ridiculous things! Are you touched by Satan?" thundered Brother Simon.

"No, just being truthful." She smiled at me, and her smile was more like Potiphar's wife than a minister's wife.

Brother Simon pointed at his large house. "Ashley Sue! Home! Obey me."

Ashley Sue gave me another sexy smile, then turned and walked home. Brother Simon didn't notice, but I sure did: Ashley Sue was walking away with a definite hip-sway.

Brother Simon stepped forward and shoved a finger in my face. "See what you've done? These immoral women whom you've brought here have brought moral decay with them."

I replied, "Word of advice: Don't wave a finger in the face of someone who's pulled more than his share of engines, unless you plan to lose that finger."

Not trusting myself further around this blowhard, I turned my back on him, walked back to my mower, and started it up. Brother Simon yelled something, but the mower noise drowned it out.

To Gothika's annoyance, I did not accept a blowjob from her as soon as I finished mowing and bagging the grass. I showered, then I ran errands, then the ladies and I went grocery-shopping. Oh, the envious stares I got! Then came the women fixing dinner, and all of us eating it.

Then Sarah and Slave Deborah went to work, while Ashley and Slave Jeanette washed dishes. By the time I was sitting in the recliner and Ashley was slurping my cock, the sun had set and I could just barely see into my back yard.

Slave Jeanette startled. "Someone's in your back yard!" She took several steps toward my sliding-glass door. "It's a teenage girl walking a bicycle."

"*What?*" I said. I tried to stand up—no easy thing when a woman has my cock in her mouth. "Let me up," I ordered Gothika, and—after two more slurps—she did.

As I was tucking my cock in my pants, Gothika muttered, "Shit! The blowjob doesn't count if it's stopped halfway through."

Seconds later, the automatically activated porch light revealed Ashley Lynn standing at my sliding-glass door. As she knocked on the glass, she was pulling a knapsack off her shoulder.

Slave Jeanette pulled open the door a few inches, and spoke quietly to Ashley Lynn. Then Slave Jeanette turned to me and said, "She says she needs help with her geometry." Ashley Lynn, meanwhile, was looking pleadingly at me through the glass.

I gestured for Ashley Lynn to enter; as soon as she was inside, I asked, "Why are you asking *me* for help, instead of somebody in your class?"

She said, "I fibbed to your roommate. I'm here so that you'll, um, take my cherry. I hope I've waited long enough." Again she looked pleadingly at me. "Mom and Father think I'm at Debbie Barrett's house."

Shit, my Power strikes again. "You're offering me your virginity? Out of the question—go home!"

Ashley Lynn shook her head. "Mister Hanson, my first time, it's gotta be with you, right here." Then she glanced down at Gothika and back in my eyes. "Mister Hanson, um, I know it's none of my business, um, but was she giving you, um, a *you-know*?"

Considering that Gothika was kneeling more-or-less in front of the recliner, my face was flushed, and my cock inside my shorts was erect, I couldn't very well lie. "Yeah, something like that," I replied to Ashley Lynn.

She bit her lip. "I've never kissed a boy's thing before. So my first time for *that* has to be with you too."

"Bullshit!" cried Gothika, who was standing up from her kneeling position. "You're not getting your cherry mouth anywhere near Tim's cock till he's come in *my* mouth. Got it, girlie?"

I tried to recover the discussion. "Child, I don't know why you're pushing me about your virginity, but it's no go. Period, end of discussion, the end."

"But you told me to!" said Ashley Lynn. "You said, 'Ashley, wait till later for that first one here. I'm not interested in getting sexy with you right now.' "

I tried using what I'd learned with Susie, about changing a prior Power command. "Ashley Lynn, when I said that, I didn't mean you. I was talking—"

"—to me," said Gothika. "The woman also known as Ashley Holly Baker." Gothika then put on a Southern accent and added, "But if any of y'all call me 'Ashley Holly,' you will dah a slow and painful dayuth."

Meanwhile, I was looking at Ashley Lynn, expecting her to pick up her knapsack, mutter blushing apologies, and flee. Instead, she said, "Can we f—boink now, or do I got to wait some more? And can one of you teach me how to . . . kiss his thing?"

I was wracking my brains, trying to figure out a way to outsmart my Power, when Slave Jeanette spoke up. "Tim, I think you should do it. Take her cherry."

Ashley Lynn looked at Slave Jeanette with a hopeful expression; Gothika and I looked at Slave Jeanette as if she were a Martian. "How do you figure that?" I asked.

Slave Jeanette replied, "*You* not only make a woman's body feel good, you make her heart feel good too. Special. Desired. And good or bad, every woman remembers her first fuck."

"How old are you?" Gothika asked Ashley Lynn.

"Eighteen and three months. And twenty-two days," Ashley Lynn told me.

"Still a virgin at eighteen?" Slave Jeanette said. "Poor child."

Gothika smiled at me. "She's legal." Then Gothika knelt in front of me again, saying, "But I wasn't kidding. I have a promise to keep, and nobody's getting near Tim till I keep it." Then Gothika yanked down my shorts, and then grabbed my cock with her mouth.

Ever been sucked-off by a motivated and expert cocksucker, while a teen virgin watches you with an expression that combines amazement and lust? It seemed like mere seconds before I was thrusting my hips and moaning.

"She's swallowing all his man-juice," Slave Jeanette explained to Ashley Lynn. "Boys *really, really* like it when a girl does that. But a girl who refuses to, is a tease and a bitch." Ashley Lynn nodded, but her eyes never left Gothika's bobbing head.

When Gothika finally pulled her mouth off my happy cock, and I was putting my cock back in my pants again, the doorbell rang.

––––––––––––––

For the second time in an hour, I had to hurry to stuff my Gothika-sucked dick back in my pants. I opened the front door. Standing there was Ashley Lynn's mother (and Brother Simon's wife), Ashley Sue.

Ashley Sue looked relieved to see me. "Timothy!"

I said, "I don't know how you found her, but she's here," as I opened the door and gestured Ashley Sue inside.

She looked confused. "Who is 'her'?"

"Um, hi, Mom," said Ashley Lynn.

"Honey, why are you here and not at Debbie's?"

Ashley Lynn began, "Well, I couldn't understand the lecture in geometry—"

I spun around. *"What?"*

As soon as I looked into the girl's eyes, she said, "Actually, Mom, I came here to get my first times with Mister Hanson. To do, you know, *sex stuff.*"

Ashley Sue gasped. "Ashley Lynn, are you turning into a *slut*? After all that your father and I have done for you?"

But before the daughter could answer the mother's question, the mom herself got put on the spot: Gothika asked, "If you didn't know your daughter was here, why did you come here?"

"To invite everyone. . ." Ashley Sue stammered when I made eye contact with her. "Um, I told Simon that I was going here to invite everyone to our church next Sunday. And y'all are. Invited, I mean. But mainly. . ."

By now, Ashley Sue's cheeks were red. The minister's respectable wife took a breath, looked me in the eyes, and said, "Mainly, I came here to have sex with you here, Timothy, like I've never had before." Behind me, Ashley Lynn gasped.

What was I supposed to do now? Fucking a minister's wife— not to mention the minister's virgin teen daughter—seemed to me wrong, wrong, wrong. But I couldn't negate my Power in this, so my choices were either to enjoy both Ashleys, or watch them go straitjacket-crazy.

Behind me, Ashley Lynn asked, "Mister Hanson, does this mean you'll get naked now?"

Chapter 15
Two Ashleys' First Times

In my living room, Ashley Sue looked at me and said, "Mainly, I came here to have sex with you, Timothy, like I've never had before." Behind me, Ashley Lynn gasped.

Then Ashley Lynn asked, "Mister Hanson, does this mean you'll get naked now?"

"Come in my bedroom, both of you," I said. "We need to talk."

" 'Talk'? Is *that* what you call it?" Gothika said.

I started to walk toward my bedroom. At that, Ashley Sue raised a hand and glared at her daughter. "Young lady, you don't need to be a part of this. You go home right this instant."

"Why? So you can cheat on Father without me seeing it? It's still adultery." Ashley Lynn was dressed like a goody-two-shoes, but right now she showed the rebellious face of a teen runaway.

"Ashley Sue, Ashley Lynn," I said, "follow me, both of you." I walked into my bedroom and both Effib women joined me there. Once in the bedroom, I said to them, "Ashley Sue, Ashley Lynn, each of you accept that you have a sexual need to be here and that the other one also needs to be here. Even if you don't understand it, accept it." They both nodded, and their tense postures relaxed.

But then Ashley Sue pointed to a twin mattress that was lying in a corner. "Why is there both a king-sized bed and a twin mattress in your bedroom?"

I had not shut my bedroom door, and so Gothika and Slave Jeanette were standing outside my doorway, watching and listening. Now Slave Jeanette replied, "That's my bed. I sleep there when I'm not fucking Tim."

"You treat her like a dog?" Ashley Lynn asked me. The girl's expression was a mixture of outrage, curiosity, and excitement.

Gothika laughed. "First of all, Jen-Jen is *my slave*—she doesn't rate a four-poster bed. Secondly, Tim's girlfriend and *his* slave girl aren't here right now."

"I'm sorry?" Ashley Sue said to Gothika. "You have a slave, Timothy has a slave, *and* Timothy has a girlfriend?"

The mother had asked the question, but Gothika replied to the daughter: "Let that be a lesson to you. If you ever start shaking your naked boobs in guys' faces on the job, one day you'll be doing kinky shit off the job."

I said, "To clarify what Gothika said: My bed sleeps three, it doesn't sleep four. When Sarah and Slave Deborah are here, they sleep with me. So ordinarily, Slave Jeanette can't fit on my bed. Hence, the mattress there."

Ashley Lynn crossed her arms and tapped her foot. "This is all interesting, but *we're in your bedroom.* Do we get naked now? Are we about to *do sex stuff?*"

"Yes, in a minute," I replied.

I'd realized that if these two Ashleys were magically compelled to have sex with me (and would go crazy if they didn't), it was my moral duty to have sex with both of them. Besides, this whole situation had me steel-hard again.

"In a minute, I will have sex with you, young lady," I basically told Ashley Lynn. But then I looked at her mother and added, "But first I need to know what exactly *you* expect from me, when I romp with *you.*"

Ashley Sue said, "It has to be sex, with you, of a type I've never done before. I've never cheated on my husband before, so Timothy, I want you to fuck me till I scream."

"You've never cheated on Hubby?" Gothika asked. "But surely you've *wanted* to, hm?"

"Of course not, never," Ashley Sue snapped. But then she caught my glance, and she said, "Except when I found out that my husband was screwing Mary Bell. Then I felt like walking naked into a frat house."

Ashley Lynn's eyebrows shot up. "Mary Bell, the Choir Director? *Our* Mary Bell?"

"Uh-huh. So now you understand why I haven't sent her a Christmas card for three years now."

I said to Ashley Sue, "I'm not comfortable with fucking you, since you're married. What about oral sex? Is that something you've never done before?"

"Oh, please. Simon made me suck his cock on our wedding night. Nowadays I have to blow him at least three times a week, Mary Bell or no Mary Bell." She turned to her daughter and added, " 'Be ye submissive to your husbands' means that if he wants a blowjob, he gets a blowjob."

Ashley Lynn shuddered. "Too much information, Mom!"

Ashley Sue shrugged. "Could be worse. Thank God, your father isn't into—"

"Don't say it, Ashley Sue!" I told her. I wasn't about to butt-fuck a minister's virgin daughter. But if anyone mentioned anal sex around Ashley Lynn, she would be compelled to add it to her list of "first times" with me.

Then I returned to the earlier topic. "What about cunnilingus?" I asked Ashley Sue. "What kinds have you received before?"

"Cunni-*what?*"

"Pussy-licking," I explained. "The woman receiving oral sex."

She looked at me in puzzlement. "Isn't that what lesbians do?"

"So in all the time you've been married, Simon has never licked your pussy?"

Again I got a puzzled look. "How could he? He's not a lesbian."

I covered my eyes with my hand. "Slave Jeanette, explain birds, bees, and tuna tacos to Ashley Sue," I said.

Slave Jeanette smiled at me and said to Ashley Sue, "It's not just wild women who lick pussies. *Most* men do it too. In fact, Tim is talented."

"Ooh, I *gotta* try that!" Ashley Lynn exclaimed. "Please, Mister Hanson, can we? *Please?*"

"Me too?" Ashley Sue said.

I said, "It looks like we have the agenda for the three-way worked out." I began unbuttoning my shirt.

"Um, Mister Hanson?" Ashley Lynn squeaked. "Will *they* be. . .?" She was looking at my stripper housemates.

My hands left my shirt. I smacked my forehead, then walked to the doorway of my bedroom. Slave Jeanette was grinning; Gothika was smirking. I said, "Go watch some DVDs of 'The L Word.' Nothing to see here." Then I shut my bedroom door.

I turned to the girl. "Ashley Lynn, I'm going to make love to your mother before I have sex with you. I know you have questions, but some of them will get answered if you watch carefully."

Then I turned to the other woman there, who looked nervous. "Ashley Sue Effib," I said, "enjoy all this, and don't worry about what anyone sees you doing here." Then I kissed her, long and slow.

Ashley Lynn remarked, "Mom, your nipples have gotten pointy."

"It means his kiss is getting me hot," Ashley Sue said, in a husky voice. Then she stepped back and reached for the buttons on her blouse.

"Nuh-uh," I said. "Undressing you is *my* job." I began to unbutton her blouse.

"Oh my," she said. "The last time I was undressed by a man was my honeymoon."

The shirttails of her blouse were tucked into her skirt. After I'd unbuttoned her blouse and as I was pulling the blouse free, I said, "Ashley Sue, you deserve better from Simon than you're getting." Neither mother nor daughter made reply.

Two minutes later, I had Ashley Sue bare to the waist, and I was sucking on a nipple. She enjoyed that: "Oh my. Oh my. *Ohh,* that feels good."

Ashley Lynn asked, "Mom, why do you have your eyes closed?"

"Because, anything I see is a distraction right now. Timothy, that is very nice."

The room was getting pungent with the smell of aroused female. After I unzipped Ashley Sue's skirt and pushed it down to the floor, I moved my hand inside her panties. "You're wet," I said.

"So am I, Mister Hanson," Ashley Lynn said. "I'm really wanting for someone to touch me where you're touching Mom."

I hugged Ashley Sue close to me with my left arm, while my right hand delighted her pussy and clit. Meanwhile, I turned to Ashley Lynn and said, "Young lady, you have a choice. You can wait a half-hour or an hour till it's your turn with me, or else you can take matters in hand."

"I'll try to hold off, Mister Hanson. But I'm totally horny."

By now I'd undressed the mother completely, and I was leading her to my bed. But I glanced over at Ashley Lynn and said, "Congratulations, girl. You've finally spoken a word that wasn't Sunday School approved."

I lay down with Ashley Sue. I kissed her on the lips, while I played with her pussy. Then I got on top of her, kissing her body. I treated her torso like a ski run: I kissed to the right, and I licked to the left, but always I was moving in one overall direction.

By the time that Ashley Sue's pubic hair was stroking my chin, she was moaning and writhing, and she reeked of pussy juice.

I pushed myself up, looked Ashley Sue in the eyes, and asked, "Are you ready to receive your first pussy-licking?"

"*Do it!*"

I did. Her hips came right off the bed when my tongue touched her clit, and she screamed till she gasped for air. Beyond my bedroom door sounded whistles and applause.

I licked Ashley Sue's pussy, and sucked on her clit, for a good long time. She really liked my trick of pushing a finger in her pussy, and both my thumb and my tongue stroking her clit at the same time.

Did she enjoy the time I spent licking her? Let me put it this way: I found myself wishing I'd brought a golf counter to bed. Did she orgasm so hard, and so often, because I was great at cunnilingus? Perhaps. Or perhaps Ashley Sue climaxed so well because she was so psyched up beforehand.

When I rolled off Ashley Sue and looked at the clock, forty-five minutes had passed.

"How *was* it, Mom?"

"Daughter, it was *wondrous*. Timothy, thank you, thank you."

I climbed off the bed, looked at Ashley Lynn, and smiled. "I'm ready for you now, but I think you'd prefer for me to first wash my face and brush my teeth."

"Please don't take too long, Mister Hanson, okay?"

"Okay, but no more 'Mister Hanson' while you're sucking my cock or I'm fucking you. Ashley Lynn, Ashley Sue, if sex is done right, we're equals."

When I stepped out of the master bathroom, I saw that Ashley Sue had pulled her panties back on. But she was making no effort to dress further. It isn't often I see a topless minister's wife.

I walked up to Ashley Lynn and put my hands on her girlish shoulders. "Are you ready to fuck away your cherry, suck cock, and get licked?"

"*Shit yeah*, Tim!" the virginal minister's daughter replied.

"Language, young lady," Ashley Sue said. But she was smiling.

"Here we go, Ashley Lynn," I said. Then I kissed her. "Now I'm going to undress you."

Minutes later, I had Ashley Lynn bare to the waist. She had great-looking skin that was also soft to the touch. Her tits were almost as big as her mother's, and the girl's "girls" had no sag to them. "Great tits," I said.

Ashley Lynn smiled big. "You really think so?"

"Shit yeah, Ashley Lynn!" I said. All three of us laughed. I was cupping both teenaged tits at the time, tugging at the nipples, so I knew that both Ashleys knew I was sincere.

Ashley Sue stepped forward. "Now, honey, do to him what he did to you: Undress him to the waist." Seconds later, the mother was telling the daughter, "That's it, whenever you see skin of his, caress it. It'll get both of you hot."

Seconds later, I said, "Your mom is right, you know. Look, it's gotten bigger and harder." I was talking about the cock-bulge in my pants.

Ashley Lynn looked down, and her eyes got big. "Can I touch it?"

"Sure, in a little bit, you can touch it naked. But for right now, rub the front of my pants."

"Oh, it's like wood! Or steel."

"And you made me that way."

"Wow."

" 'Wow' is right," Ashley Sue murmured.

I sat Ashley Lynn on the edge of my bed, and pulled off her shoes and knee-high stockings. She returned the favor with my shoes and socks. Then I said, "Before I remove your skirt, I want you to remove my pants."

She nodded and de-pantsed me. Then I "discovered" that when my pants were around my ankles, I needed her help to step out of them. She squatted down so that I could use her shoulder as a cane. Which by the way, put her face only inches from my boxers-covered dick. You better believe I had a boner.

Ashley Lynn's eyes were wide. "Ooh, do we have to wait till we're both naked to take the next step? Help me, Mom."

"Hold on a sec," I said. I walked to the nightstand by my bed, my erection swaying inside my boxers; seconds later, I returned holding a foil-wrapped condom.

Standing in front of Ashley Lynn, I gave her a sex-ed lecture—nearly naked, and with a hard-on:

"We guys *hate* putting on a condom. But Ashley Lynn, believe me when I tell you that we'll always put one on when you make it clear that our choices are 'wear a condom' or 'no sex.' But guys will try to argue you away from that ultimatum; we'll say, 'I'm clean.' Ashley Lynn, believe me: Some guys will say they're clean when they think they're not, and a few shitheads will swear they're clean when they *know* they're not."

Ashley Sue asked, "Are *you* clean?"

"I haven't been tested since last month," I replied. I didn't mention that before I got the Power, I'd been living like a monk, so who needs disease testing? I continued, "I'm currently involved with five women, seven counting you two—"

"*Seven?*" Ashley Sue echoed.

"—so if you and I had done anything other than cunnilingus, you better believe I'd have worn a condom." I turned back to her daughter and said, "When you and I fuck, I'll wear a condom. Besides not giving you a disease if I have one, nobody here wants my tadpoles hooking up with your basketball."

"Thank you," both Ashleys said.

"Blowjobs are a special case," I continued, "Not only does the man hate to wear a condom during a blowjob, but the woman dislikes it too—"

"Amen," said Ashley Sue.

"But if I don't put on a condom, you run the risk of catching something. So what do you choose for me to do?"

Ashley Sue and Ashley Lynn shared glances, then Ashley Lynn said to me, "This first time, I want to taste you naked. Mom, what do I do now?"

"Pull his shorts down, honey, and help him step out of them." When Ashley Lynn had done that to me, Ashley Sue continued, "Now get your nose close to him. Smell him."

"His cock smells weird, Mom. I can't decide if I like the smell or not."

"Some women like the smell, some don't. Now, stick out your tongue and lick whatever of his cock you can reach."

"Oh, that's *ni-i-i-ice*," I said.

"See, honey? He likes that. Now take the head in your mouth, and slide your lips down the shaft and up again. Uh-huh, do it again, down and back, like it's a warm Popsicle."

"Teeth, teeth!" I yelped. "No teeth!"

"Open your jaws a little, honey," Ashley Sue. "Keep your lips on his cock, but don't scrape him with your teeth."

"That feels good," I said. "You should know that—oh yeah, Ashley Lynn, just like that—if you speed up, you get me off sooner, but if you go slow, my orgasm is more intense when I finally do come."

Ashley Sue said, "But you should know that if you go fast, muscles get tired. But if you take a long time to get him off, your knees and jaws and lips start hurting."

Five seconds later, Ashley Lynn speeded up to pogo-stick speed. Maybe thirty seconds later, I gasped, "I'm going to shoot."

Ashley Sue said, "I never let your father come in my mouth, honey."

But Ashley Lynn didn't change anything, except to speed up even more. I couldn't help it, I started moaning—it was a better blowjob than I was expecting, and I was getting it from an innocent virgin while her mother advised her. The situation was too hot for me to stay calm.

I lost control; I spurted. Ashley Lynn whimpered when my cum first hit her throat. I gasped, "Your choices now are to spit it out when I finish cumming—"

"MMM-mmm," Ashley Lynn said, while still mouth-fucking me.

"—or start swallowing what comes out. I can't control my ejaculate. I would really like it if you keep milking me till my cock gets small and soft."

She didn't spit, and she didn't stop. She did, however, slow down. I could learn to like ministers' daughters.

A minute later, I said, "You can stop now." She had a little trouble getting up off her knees. When she was standing, we French-kissed. Then she smiled at me and asked hopefully, "So was I good?"

"Girl, you have a talent," I said.

Ashley Sue asked, "Why did you suck him off and swallow him?"

"Because the strawberry blonde told me earlier that girls who don't swallow are cockteasers and bitches."

Ashley Sue looked at me and asked, "Is that what *you* think, Timothy?"

I said, "My feeling is, sucking off a man and not swallowing is like baking him a cake but not putting frosting on it—why make the effort if you plan to give him only half the enjoyment? Of course, if he's twisting your arm to get that blowjob in the first place, managing his orgasm is a good compromise, I suppose."

She frowned. "You never force women to give you blowjobs?"

"You remember Gothika, the third Ashley? What do you think she'd do if I pushed her to her knees and demanded, 'Service me, woman'? She'd castrate me with her teeth. But trust me, when she sucks my dick of her own free will, she makes my spine melt."

I felt a tug on my arm. I turned to look at Ashley Lynn, who asked, "So really truly honest, you liked my blowjob? I did good?"

"Yes, Ashley Lynn, you should be proud of your blowjob technique."

"YES!" she exclaimed. I must say, a fist-pump is an interesting thing to see, when done by a bare-breasted teen girl.

I then said, "Just remember in the future, Ashley Lynn, 'No teeth.' "

Then I said, "Now it's time to pay you back, girl, oral for oral." Ashley Lynn's nipples got hard. I bent down and sucked on those nipples, which made her start breathing hard.

I removed her skirt. I sat her on the edge of my bed and pulled off her panties. Her pussy was wet, and its odor was strong.

I knelt by the bed, draped her legs over my shoulders, and then I started licking her pussy up and down.

She gasped, she moaned, and she thrashed around.

Just as her mother had, Ashley Lynn loved it when I sucked on her clit. The girl's response was "OH MY GOD, MOM! OH WOW, OH MY GOD!"

And then she grabbed my head and pulled it against her crotch. She made a long-lasting, high-pitched, wordless sound as she came a second time.

I pulled Ashley Lynn up my bed to where her head lay on my pillow, and then I lay on top of her. I had not kissed the mother except briefly, but I necked with the daughter, groping her tits and pussy while I was kissing her.

Then I stopped kissing her to say, "You enjoyed your pussy-licking, didn't you? But wait, there's more!"

I gave Ashley Lynn a peck on the lips, then began a ski run down her torso. I kissed the girl the same way the girl had seen me kiss her mother.

Ashley Lynn moaned and writhed when my head got near her crotch again.

Then I heard a slurpy sound to my left. I glanced over, and discovered that Ashley Sue had a hand busy in her panties as she watched me pleasure her daughter. I thought, *My Power strikes again.*

Thirty minutes later, Ashley Lynn was more than ready. As she lay on the bed, she watched wide-eyed as I condomed my cock. Then I got on top of her, looked in her eyes, and said, "This is the last minute of your virginity."

She said, "I'm ready, but your face smells like, you know, pussy."

"Washing my face *now* would ruin the moment. This problem will come up again in your life, by the way."

She shrugged. "Then fuck me now, Mist—fuck me, Tim. Put your cock in my pussy."

I did—or I tried to. I got the tip in, and it hit an obstruction. I pushed with my hips, broke through the obstruction, and Ashley

Lynn gasped. It was not a gasp of delight, but of pain. She clutched me with a painful grip.

Ashley Sue said, "Timothy, can you not move till she stops hurting? Honey, it only hurts for a little while."

After thirty seconds or so, Ashley Lynn nodded to me. I fucked her slowly. She made several grimaces of pain, and I felt something in her pussy scrape against my dick.

Her face relaxed, as the scraping sensation disappeared. Soon after that, she smiled at me. Soon after *that*, her pussy got wet again.

Have I mentioned that I love a tight pussy?

"Ohh, Tim, you make me feel so good," Ashley Lynn told me. She lifted up her head and kissed me.

Soon after, she said, "Oh Mom, I could really get used to this. Now I understand why Father preaches against it."

Now she was breathing hard. She started thrusting her hips to match my own thrusts, saying, "This is good, oh yeah, so good, that's it, oh yeah, like that. . ."

Meanwhile, in my head I was saying the Pledge of Allegiance backward and reciting state capitals, just so I wouldn't pop-off before Ashley Lynn had *lots* of fun.

Soon she was breathing hard, like Darth Vader's sister. "I'm close, Tim. You're getting me close, I'm so—I like this, I like this, oh yeah. . ."

I said, "Come for me, Ashley Lynn. I want to give you your first fucking orgasm."

She kissed me again. "I feel—oh, I've never—oh yes, oh god, here it comes, almost, almost, *oh god, oh god, YESSSSS!*"

Her arms tightened her grip on my torso. Her hip-thrusts got frantic, and then she froze in place with hips upthrust. She made loud and unintelligible noises.

I felt very proud of myself. Five minutes later, I was proud of myself again.

I'm told that it's unusual for a girl to climax, the first time she is fucked. Well, either I'm an unusually good lover, or my Power was in action again. Ashley Lynn came twice when I fucked her;

and of course she'd already climaxed 3,746 times while I'd eaten her out.

And if *I* was surprised that Ashley Lynn climaxed twice while she was getting fucked for the first time, Ashley Lynn's mother was flat-out *amazed*.

After I got out of bed, I trashed the condom, washed my face, and brushed my teeth; and by then, the Ashleys were mostly dressed. After I myself got dressed, I gave the mother a long, slow kiss, then I did the same for the daughter. Then we walked out of my bedroom.

In the living room, Gothika and Slave Jeanette were watching that morning's Ellen Show. When Gothika saw Ashley Sue, the lesbian stripper grinned at the minister's wife and said, "Sex is a lot more fun when you don't follow the rules, isn't it?"

Ashley Sue's face showed realization. "You're right, staying respectable gets in the way of great sex."

Ashley Lynn said, "I don't know what great sex is yet, but my pussy is happy. You two are *totally* lucky that Tim can fuck you every day."

Gothika said, "He doesn't fuck me, he fucks Jen-Jen here. She's half hetero—not that there's anything wrong with that."

"I'm confused," Ashley Sue said. "You're a stripper, with huge implants. How can you be a lesbian?"

"I was born a lesbian, but I choose to be a stripper, and I chose to get implants. But back to Tim—if I ever decide to fuck a guy again, Tim will be that guy."

"I love you too, Ashley Holly Baker," I said.

Chapter 16
Invited To Church

The next few days were uneventful. I made a new commercial and, as I'd promised Gothika, she had a part in it. A *big* part, actually—

```
A distraught motorist (SUSAN) and her car
(with the hood up) are in front of a deal-
ership's service bay. In the background is
a sign that says "BRANDEX MOTORS--YOU'LL
TELL EVERYONE ABOUT US."

Talking to Susan is a female mechanic who
is wearing coveralls with the top two snaps
unsnapped. Her name-patch reads "Bertha,"
but it is really ASHLEY.

Susan has a purse hanging from her down-
stage shoulder. Ashley has a calculator in
a pocket of her coveralls.

SUSAN: So what's wrong with it?

ASHLEY: It needs a gold-plated defibrilla-
tor. The factory, only place I can get your
part.

SUSAN (close to panic): How much to fix it?
```

Ashley pulls the calculator from her pocket and punches in numbers. Ashley looks Susan up and down, smiles evilly, and punches in more numbers. Ashley shows the calculator result to Susan.

SUSAN: That's more money than I have!

ASHLEY: Really? How much do you got?

Not waiting for Susan to answer, Ashley yanks Susan's purse off her shoulder, opens the purse, and dumps the contents on the ground. Ashley drops the purse itself into an oil puddle. (NOTE: The puddle's "motor oil" is actually chocolate sauce.)

Ashley bends forward to see what was in Susan's purse. (NOTE: If Ashley's cover-alls' third snap wasn't snapped, this commercial would be showing lots of fine cleavage and wouldn't be family-friendly anymore.)

ASHLEY: You don't have enough money, sure enough.

INSERT: There are only a few green bills on the ground. BACK TO:

ASHLEY (leering at Susan): Girlie, you're completely at my mercy.

SFX: TOW-TRUCK HORN, ONE LONG AND THREE SHORT

Backing up to Brandex Motors' service bay is a TIM HANSON FORD tow truck.

INSERT: Painted on the driver's door of the tow truck is text, "TIM HANSON FORD." BACK TO:

The tow truck stops, and SARAH and DEBORAH get out.

Sarah and Deborah rush over to Susan and each give her a quick hug.

(While everyone else is talking, the tow truck is hooking up Susan's car so that it can be towed away. Deborah is picking up the cash lying on the ground.)

SUSAN (to Sarah): My car needs a gold-plated defibrillator.

SARAH: There's no such thing! They're trying to cheat you.

DEBORAH: We're taking your car to Tim Hanson Ford, because he has the No Cheat Guarantee.

SUSAN: What's this No Cheat Guarantee?

SARAH: If anyone at Tim Hanson Ford tries to cheat you, the owner fires the cheater then and there.

SUSAN: That will be a load off my mind.

ASHLEY: You can't leave yet. She still owes us sixty bucks.

Deborah pulls out three bills from the cash she's picked up. But instead of handing the bills to Ashley, Deborah drops the bills on the ground by the "oil puddle."

Ashley bends down to pick up the cash. She's facing the "oil puddle."

Sarah puts a foot on Ashley's butt, and pushes. Ashley lands face-first in the "oil puddle."

INSERT: Ashley lifts her face up from the puddle. Her face is covered with gooey brown liquid. BACK TO:

Susan, Sarah, and Deborah get in the tow-truck cab.

INSERT: The tow-truck passenger door shuts, and so we can read its text, "TIM HANSON FORD." BACK TO:

The tow truck leaves, pulling Susan's car.

SUSAN (OS): Tell me where we're going.

DEBORAH (OS): Tim Hanson Ford is on Smith Freeway northbound, a quarter-mile north of the Woodrow Wilson exit.

INSERT: Tim Hanson is in his dealership office.

TIM HANSON: My name is Timothy Richard
Hanson, and if anyone at my dealership
cheats you, they will be fired on the spot!
I guarantee it.

I had "entertained" the Ashleys Effib on Monday night. On Wednesday night, my doorbell rang. Standing outside my front door was Brother Simon, his wife and daughter, and another woman.

Standing behind her father, Ashley Lynn looked confused. Something was going on, but the girl hadn't figured out what.

"Yes, can I help you?" I said warily to Brother Simon.

Ashley Sue was trying to catch my eye, as if she was trying to silently pass on a message. But I couldn't figure out what she was trying to say. Also, I noticed that Ashley Sue looked sexier somehow—something about her makeup was different.

Brother Simon said, "Mr. Simon, you know my wife and daughter. This is Mary Bell, our church Choir Director. May we come in?"

One of the rules that good salesmen know is, *Take charge of the relationship.* So you better believe I spotted what Brother Simon was trying to pull. I replied, "No, I'll just step outside instead."

As I shut the front door behind me, I said to Brother Simon, "I ask again: How can I help you?"

Brother Simon's bad attitude of Monday was completely gone. "Mister Hanson, I'm giving a special sermon at our ten o'clock Sunday service, about something of special interest to you. So I'm extending a *special* invitation for you to attend our service."

"Simon, that is nice of you, but Saturday is big at the dealership, and so I work till late Saturday night. I always sleep late on Sunday morn—"

"Mister Hanson, I can understand why you're saying no. I acted nasty and immature the other day."

"Simon, you were all that and more. Thanks for admitting you were wrong. But I wasn't kidding about Sunday morning, I *need* that time to recover."

Ashley Sue took a breath. "Timothy—"

Brother Simon whipped his head around. "Ashley Sue! You don't need to speak here. Let Mary and me handle this." Then he turned to me, all smiles again. "Mister Hanson—"

"Mister Hanson," Mary Bell said, "I'm *very much* hoping that you will come to the service."

Brother Simon frowned. I thought, *Aha, Mary Bell is going off-script. The plot thickens.*

I turned to Mary and said, "It's nice of you also to ask, but the answer is still no."

As I spoke, I looked Mary Bell over. She was clothed modestly, but that was where the modesty stopped. She was looking at me in a sexual way, sending me a "For a good time, call" vibe. Which she was good at—porn actresses take classes to learn how to pout like that. She was a bottle blonde; and while her tits weren't as big as a stripper's, they were bigger than average.

Was Mary Bell wanting to hook up with me? Or was she trying to lure me into something? I couldn't say. And what was Brother Simon's game? I decided I didn't want to know.

I looked at Brother Simon, as I reached for the front door. "If you'll excuse me—"

"Would it help if I beg? *Please*, Mr. Hanson, come. And if you can, bring your, uh, houseguests."

I glanced at Ashley Lynn, who shrugged. Ashley Sue was again trying to beam thoughts into my head—unsuccessfully. Brother Simon watched my face. Mary Bell's expression, I couldn't read.

Brother Simon continued, "But bring yourself to our Sunday ten o'clock service, I beg you."

Oh, hell. What kind of heartless bastard would I be if a man was reduced to begging me for something, and I told him no anyway? I sighed and said, "Okay, fine. Ten a.m., I'll be there. But I might be yawning."

Brother Simon, smiling, turned to Mary Bell. "Did you hear that, Mary? He told us all he'd be there Sunday."

She nodded. "I heard him."

He turned back to me, and thanked me, smiling all the while. But his smile was *off*, somehow.

I glanced at Ashley Sue. At last I could read her face's unspoken message: *You poor fool.*

Why? I would go to a church service—there'd be some singing, an offering taken, and a sermon. What could go wrong?

Chapter 17
I'm Told I Was Tricked

The next morning, after the Morning Meeting, I was talking to Betty Jane in my office when Susie burst in. Susie said, "Mister Hanson, there's a call holding for you. Says it's urgent."

"Tell him I'll pick up in a few minutes." I could say that because we weren't open yet. I asked, "Customer, vendor, or employee?"

"It's your neighbor"—Susie looked down at the paper— "Ashley Lynn Effib, and she insisted that she has to talk to you *right this minute.*"

Oh, shit, I thought. Aloud, I said, "Betty Jane, looks like we'll have to continue this in your office in a few minutes."

After Betty Jane and Susie left, I picked up my phone. "Hello, Tim Hanson here."

Ashley Lynn said, "Hi, uh, Tim? I'm gonna be late for Second Period, can't talk long. It's about my dad."

I got a sick feeling in my stomach, but my voice was calm. "What about your dad?"

"Yesterday afternoon, he was asking me all sorts of questions about Monday. Remember how I lied to him, said I was going to Debbie Barrett's to study? Yesterday afternoon he was asking me about that, over and over. What we studied, when I got to Debbie's house, when I left, conversations we had, the whole nine yards. I did *serious* lying."

"And he asked the same stuff over and over, like in cop shows? Like he was trying to catch you in a lie?"

"Uh-huh. When he doesn't believe what I'm saying, he does this thing with his eyebrow, you know? Yesterday he tried to hide it, but twice while I was talking to him, he did the eyebrow thing."

"So does he know that Monday night, I had sex with you and your mom?"

"Does he *know*? He's acting that way, but I don't see how. Believe me, *I* sure didn't tell him, and I can't imagine that Mom would tell him anything."

"Thanks for the heads-up, Ashley Lynn. I'd better let you go."

"Tim, one more thing?"

"Yes?"

"You *rock* between the sheets! Seriously."

An hour later, the other shoe dropped—Ashley Sue called me. The first words out of her mouth were, "Timothy, I messed up."

"Messed up how?"

"Tuesday night, after I gave Simon his blowjob, I asked him to lick my pussy."

"I thought you had never done that before."

"Nope, never have. But Tuesday, I was blowing him and I thought, *He owes me.* So when I could talk again, I asked him to lick me. He said, 'How can you ask me such a thing?' I said, 'Fair's fair. I did you, now you do me.' "

"What did he say to that?"

"He said, 'This is disgusting! Do not say more of this.' I said, 'Why? I deserve better than what I'm getting. Timothy says'—"

"Wait, you mentioned my name?"

"Yeah, that's where I messed up. Simon was treating me like a slave, and for some reason, that made me mad, and your name slipped out. I'm really sorry."

"It's okay. So what happened then?"

"So then he started asking me what I'd been doing Monday night. When I'd left, I'd told him I was going window-shopping. Anyway, he started cross-examining me about that. And I got mad and told him that he was making up nonsense, false accusations, just to get out of licking my pussy."

"Good for you. The best defense is a good offense."

"Then he told me that it isn't a husband's duty to 'submit' to his wife, but it's a wife's duty to submit to her husband. Including in the bedroom. And so I shot back with, 'Maybe so, maybe not, but it *is* a husband's duty to remain faithful to his wife!' "

"Whoa. It got nasty."

"Then he said, 'What do you mean by that?' I said, 'You know damn well what I mean.' I wasn't about to name names—let him worry. So he came back with 'You owe me an explanation for that last remark.' And I said, 'I don't owe you jack shit, adulterer.' "

"Whoa. So what happened last night?"

"Yesterday after Ashley Lynn got home from school, Simon was pushing her and quizzing her, like he'd done to me. Last night after dinner, I'd just started the dishwasher when the doorbell rang. It was Mary Bell. Simon fetched Ashley Lynn from upstairs, they and Mary walked into the kitchen, then Simon said, 'We're going to walk to Mister Hanson's house, all four of us, and invite him to church.' You know the rest."

"So somehow he found out what really happened Monday night. Or at least, found out enough to be suspicious."

"I can't see how."

"Did he say or do anything unusual Monday night, after you two got home?"

"No, nothing. Wait—nah, it's nothing. But it *was* unusual."

"Tell me."

"I was climbing the stairs, intending to take a shower before he smelled me, and he came to the bottom of the stairs and asked me to turn off the water faucet to the soaker hose in the front yard. He's always the one to turn off the hose before coming to bed, but Monday night he asked me to do it. He was even polite about it."

"Well, that doesn't sound like it means anything," I said.

"Probably not," Ashley Sue agreed. Then she asked me, "So now that I've told you all this, what are you going to do?"

I said, "Sometime between now and Sunday, I need to get a haircut. I'm shaggy."

"*You're still going?* But I think Simon is up to something!"

"I *know* he's up to something. But I made a promise. Ten a.m. Sunday, I'm in your church."

"Your promise, he tricked you into making that."

"Doesn't matter. I keep my promises."

The only excitement in the rest of my workday was that I slipped out to get a haircut, and talked my stylist out of buying a Honda. Hours passed, and then it was a little before 5:30 p.m.

I was just climbing out of my car in my garage, when my cel phone rang. It was Sarah calling: "Honey, I'm a ditz. I left my sack lunch on the counter. Could you bring it to the club, please, sometime before seven?"

I said, "No problem. I'll bring it now."

"You're a sweetie. I love you."

Sure enough, on the kitchen counter was an open little brown bag, with a sandwich and a baggie of carrot sticks inside, and an apple next to the bag. I bagged the apple and headed back to my car.

Some minutes later, I was walking up to the open front door of Club Nimfo. This was the first time I'd been here since the night that Mike had brought me.

In front of the door was a lectern that was painted purple and had "Club Nimfo" lettered on it in silver. Behind the lectern was a woman (young, blond, stacked, cast on her arm) who was collecting the ten-dollar cover charge. Standing next to her was a man who was huge in every way: well over six feet tall, and with enormous muscles. His biceps were like grapefruits.

I was suddenly very conscious of the fact that I had not pulled a single engine, or manhandled a single transmission, since I'd inherited the dealership.

I walked up to the lectern and held up the sack lunch. "I'm here to give Platinuma her lunch."

The big man looked at me like I was a worm. "Hey buddy, nobody gets in the frickin' club without paying the frickin' ten bucks." He had a New York or New Jersey accent.

"I don't *want* to get in the club, I just want to give Platinuma her lunch."

"I'm not saying anything more to you, I got woik to do. You wanna talk to me, you get in back of the frickin' line."

"I'm not going to pay ten—"

"Back of the frickin' line, asshole, got me?"

Seeing no alternative, I went to the back of the frickin' line. There were five guys in front of me.

When I was at the head of the line, I said, "I'm not going to stay in the club. I'm just going to talk to Platinuma for a few seconds, let her know I'm here, then hand off the lunch to the bartender."

Big Guy said, "Yeah? Well, everybody wants to talk to dis stripper or dat stripper without paying. Do you know how many notes about frickin' *dying grandmas* I seen?"

"Look, you got a walkie-talkie?"

"I'm not tellin' you jack. Maybe I do, maybe I don't."

"Can you call a manager out here, and I give the lunch to him?"

"Nope, not safe."

"Will you call a *dancer* out here, and I give the sack lunch to *her*?"

"Nope. Buddy, playtime is over—ten bucks, or take a frickin' hike."

"Fuck you," I said. "Will you at least tell me your *name*, or is *that* against frickin' policy too?"

"Vincent Cesare Capriccio."

Progress, finally. I said, "Okay, Vincent Capriccio, I ask again: You got a walkie-talkie?"

"Yeah, I got one."

"Then let's do this, Vincent Capriccio: You tell one of the bouncers inside the club that I'm coming in, and what I'm up to. And if I quit the plan, he's welcome to slam my head into the wall."

Vincent went for it. Twenty seconds later, I was entering the loud, dark strip club, a smile on my face and a ten-dollar bill still in my wallet. I waved to Slave Jeanette (a.k.a. Peachy).

I found Sarah on a stage, naked and rubbing her hands over her tits. I walked close to the stage, held up the brown sack, and jerked a thumb at the bar behind me. Sarah gave me a smile that would instantly cure erectile dysfunction.

Platinuma/Sarah was the perfect girlfriend. She was tall, platinum blond, stacked, beautiful of face, and muscle-toned; her current dance moves were pure eroticism. She was affectionate and feminine, and she let me have sex with other women. And she was *my* girlfriend, thanks to me (accidentally) using the Power that the golden god gave me. If the golden god had a temple open, I would be sending its priests a whopping tax-deductible contribution.

When I returned my thoughts to the here and now, I was walking from Sarah's stage to the bar. I noticed a giant of a man watching me. He was holding a walkie-talkie in his hand.

Walking to the bar, I also noticed my fired manager, Mike Brown, talking to redheaded dancer Sunset. Mike and Sunset weren't touching (because of club rules), but you couldn't shove a toilet-paper roll between them. Twenty to one, those two were having sex.

Mike didn't notice me, and I had no interest in talking to him. If he would be bothered by the fact that Sunset was once a man (and legally, still was a man), Mike wasn't going to find this out from me. As for Sunset, I believed that unless she were an axe murderer, she deserved a better boyfriend than Mike. But I didn't stop to tell her that.

Seconds later, the bartender was asking me, "Yes sir, what'll you have?"

I plopped the brown bag on the bar, pulled out a pen, then wrote "Platinuma" on the bag. I told the bartender, "Platinuma forgot her lunch."

A young man who was sitting nearby, spewed beer on hearing my words. "Whoa, you're banging *Platinuma*?" Then his face showed panic and he added, "Or you her brother or something?"

"I'm not her brother or something, and I am definitely banging Platinuma."

"*Wow*," he said. "Is it, you know, *good*?"

"It's the stuff of legend, guy. But I make it good for her too. That's the secret."

I was smiling as I walked away from the bar. I grinned even bigger as I walked out of Club Nimfo and past Vinnie the Mountain. But as I was getting in my car, I wondered, *Did he finally let me in the club because I wore him down, or was that somehow my Power at work?*

Friday morning, I had walked out of the bathroom and was walking by Susie's desk when she said, "There's a man waiting for you in your office."

I looked at her in amazement—even the most newbie reception-ist knows better than that. "You let a man in my office when I wasn't there? You really did that?"

She nodded, not seeing any problem. "He says he's a friend."

"That's not how a receptionist is supposed to do things, Susie."

"But he told me that it was okay for him to wait in your office, and—well, I believed it when he said that. Was I unhelpful?"

I did *not* want Susie to go into another endless-loop breakdown, so I said. "Everything's fine, I'm sure you were helpful."

When I walked into my office, standing by one of my visitor's chairs and facing me was the SUV Driver. He was even wearing the same white shirt and blue tie with white polka dots that he'd worn on the day he'd "died."

As I shook his hand, he said, "I came by to see how you—Eight planets, I never figured on any of this!"

"On any of *what*?" I asked.

"I was right about you, that you wouldn't enslave any women with your Power. Not intentionally, I mean. But by pure accident, you've built up a harem! Starting with—Cancer and Capricorn, I messed up."

"You lost me," I said. I wondered, *Do gods "mess up"?*

He sighed in relief. "I didn't think, and I set up a Contradiction Conflict within your receptionist, Susan Gloria Cooper. But already you've fixed that. Amazing. Good job."

SUV Driver stared at my forehead for several seconds. Maybe he was reading my brain, or maybe I had a ladybug crawling around up there.

Then he said, "You really are an exceptional man. You promised that priest that you will visit his temple, and so you shall, though you suspect him of bad intentions."

I smiled. "Am I right? About Brother Simon's bad intentions?"

He shrugged. "I'm a mind-reader, not omniscient. But woe unto him if he be indeed a bad priest who abuses true believers." SUV Driver walked over and slapped me on the shoulder. "You've kept your conscience throughout, and words can't describe how that pleases me. Walk me to my car?"

We walked out of my office, but then SUV Driver stopped at Susie's desk. "Susan Gloria Cooper, I thank you for believing that I am Timothy's friend. But *in the future*, it's helpful to Timothy if you keep me out here till he's ready for me."

Susie smiled big. "No problem, and I'll treat you right while you wait."

The Golden God's vehicle was the black SUV. Not only was it now unwrecked, but now it looked like it had less than a thousand miles on it. It even had a pair of Tim Hanson Ford paper license plates, which I thought was a nice touch. The Golden God shook my hand, said, "I'll see you around," then he got in the SUV and drove away.

When I came back inside, Susie said, "Your friend is a nice man."

I laughed. "Susie, you have *no* idea how nice he is."

———————

The rest of Friday and all of Saturday passed normally—minor crises and customer complaints at work, and fucks and sucks at home. Then came Sunday morning.

While I'd been driving to Brother Simon's mega-church, my cell phone had beeped: I had a text message. When I'd parked and locked my car in the church parking lot, I read the message—

I M SORRY 4 WHAT I MUST DO. OR ELSE SIMON SAYS I DIVORCED, A-L STARVE. ASHLEY SUE.

Now I was walking into Divine Blessing Cathedral.

Despite my lack of sleep, I didn't yawn as I walked inside—I was too nervous.

Chapter 18
Public Humiliation

Divine Blessing Cathedral had its own band—a drummer, two electric guitarists, a sax player, an electric fiddle player, and a trumpet player. The musicians were playing a hand-clapping song during the Offering.

The church also had two television cameras and a giant TV mounted on a side wall overhead. At the moment, the TV was switching between close-ups of one musician or another. Very likely, the overhead TV was showing us what Channel 6 was live-broadcasting to viewers throughout the metroplex.

After a while, the music stopped. Then Brother Simon stepped in front of the congregation—the audience, really—to begin his sermon. He walked out holding a book with a red-leather cover, and wearing a hands-free headset.

About this time, the image on the giant TV started flashing and twisting.

Brother Simon's amplified voice called out, "Is the car dealer Tim Hanson here? Please stand up."

I thought to myself, *Oh shit.* But as requested, I stood up.

The TV overhead cleared up and showed me in profile; I had never seen myself on TV without an automobile nearby.

"Thank you, you may sit," Brother Bob told me. As I sat down, the TV went back to fritzing up.

Brother Simon continued, "Tim Hanson is my neighbor. He's also a heir to a car dealership that he got when his father died *unexpectedly*, at an *unusually* young age."

I resent your implication! I wanted to shout.

Brother Simon continued, "Brethren and sistren, have you seen his recent commercials with the young and large-breasted women? What you don't know is, all these women live with him. . .."

Except for Susie, I mentally corrected.

". . .And Tim's house is the site of nonstop orgies. The racket that these people make, disturbs the neighbors, and the police are called repeatedly. . . ."

Another lie, I thought. *No policeman or neighbor has ever come to my door, and Sarah is quiet when she cums.*

". . .Which brings me to last Monday. Tim was cutting his grass, on a day when decent men go off to work, when I made the mistake of going to his house and inviting him to this church. I say 'mistake,' because I brought my Christian wife and Christian daughter with me. The whole time that I was talking to Tim, he was looking at my women like they were slabs of beef. Isn't that *right*, Ashley Sue?"

"Yes," I heard Ashley Sue's amplified voice say. Her voice sounded depressed and defeated. "All true."

The overhead TV cleared up its picture for two seconds, long enough to show sad Ashley Sue sitting in a pew, holding a handheld microphone. Ashley Sue's free hand was being gripped by both of the hands of a sad-looking Ashley Lynn.

Brother Simon continued, "When I returned to my house, I noticed that both my women seemed *excited*. Then a few hours later, my daughter left the house, supposedly to do homework with a girlfriend. A few minutes after that, Ashley Sue left the house, supposedly to shop. And I would have believed my wife's words, but for one thing. . . ."

Uh-oh, I thought.

". . .God has richly blessed me, so that I can afford a sunken sprinkler system around my house. But I also water my flowers the old-fashioned way, with a soaker hose. Monday at sunset, I was in my front yard when I noticed that my wife's car was parked in front of Tim Hanson's house. . . ."

Uh-oh, I thought again.

"...Two hours later, I walked down my street with a flashlight, and I found that Ashley Sue's car was still parked in front of Tim Hanson's house. . . ."

She and I are so fucked, I thought.

". . .Fifteen minutes later, both my women returned to the house—within a minute of each other. Both immediately took showers. Which then made me suspicious about my daughter, as well as my wife. . . ."

I don't like where this is going, I thought.

". . .Wednesday morning, I called the house of Ashley Lynn's supposed study partner, and talked to that girl's mother. Ashley Lynn hadn't set foot in that house, I was told."

Poor Ashley Lynn, I thought.

Then Brother Simon's voice got cheerful. "*But*, there is good news in all this. . . ."

I suspected that Brother Simon's "good news" would not be good news for *me*.

". . .Last night, my sobbing wife made a full confession, begging forgiveness. I gave that forgiveness, with my own face tear-streaked. My daughter also confessed, though with brazen pride."

What he means is: "Hey boys, my daughter is a cock-crazy slut now. Enjoy!" Ashley Lynn must have really given shit to her father.

"Talk to them, Ashley Sue," Brother Simon commanded. "Tell the people what you told me."

I glanced at the TV, and saw flickers of Ashley Sue, her head hung low, bringing the microphone to her lips. Her voice boomed from the big room's speakers: "It's true, Timothy Hansen seduced my daughter and myself. But I was weak, and let him use us."

Then a man's voice yelled from the back of the sanctuary, "ASHLEY SUE EFFIB, IF YOU'RE GOING TO SPEAK BADLY ABOUT A MAN, YOU SHOULD STAND AND FACE HIM, DON'T YOU THINK?"

Where have I heard that voice before? I wondered.

Ashley Sue slowly stood up and, with slumped shoulders, turned to face the congregation. The big television suddenly cleared up, showing Ashley Sue's defeated expression. She said, "I have sinned greatly against my husband. . ."

Then Ashley Sue's eyes found mine. Her spoken words ground to a halt.

Ashley Sue stood straighter, as her expression changed from misery to anger. "Folks, I can't lie anymore. Yes, on Monday night I had sex with Timothy Hanson. Yes, Ashley Lynn did too. But Timothy didn't smooth-talk us, he didn't trick us, he didn't force us, and *oh god*, the sex was *great!*"

Throughout the room, women gasped. Brother Simon made a throat-cut gesture, and the big television screen went black.

I pointed at the television. Ashley Sue turned around only long enough to note the dead screen, then turned back to the crowd. Her shrug meant *I'm not surprised.*

Ashley Sue continued, "My husband—Did you know 'Simon' isn't his real name?—My husband has given me only seven orgasms in twenty-two years of marriage. And five of those seven climaxes were during the first year."

"You *serpent!*" Brother Simon roared. "Be quiet with your lies!" He started to rush toward her with his hand outstretched, ready to grab the hand mike.

Then the television screen came back on, as that same mysterious male voice yelled, "BALFOUR EBENEZER EFFIB, STAY WHERE YOU ARE!"

And Brother Simon did exactly that. Oh, he put his fists on his hips and glared at his wife, but he stood fifteen feet from Ashley Sue, and now he acted uninterested in coming closer.

I noticed Ashley Sue's wide-eyed expression and the audience's murmurs only in passing. I had turned around to look behind me.

Twenty feet behind me was a television camera. Talking to that camera's cameraman was a man in his forties with a receded hairline, a white shirt, and a blue tie with white polka dots. The

SUV Driver caught my look, gave me a quick thumbs-up, and turned back to talking to the cameraman.

I turned around forward, made eye contact with Ashley Sue, and said, "You were saying?"

Ashley Sue gave me (and the TV camera) a bedroom smile. "Simon over there—I mean, *Balfour*—has given me only seven orgasms in twenty-two years. But Timothy? You gave me *more* than that, in only forty-five minutes!"

By now, Ashley Lynn was standing as well. She leaned toward the hand mike and said, "Well, *I* think I had more orgasms than Mom did! Tim, you should work as a professional Virginity Taker."

That Sunday's broadcast from the Divine Blessing Cathedral eventually went viral on YouTube. Because Ashley Sue spilled her guts over the airwaves, then Ashley Lynn came clean as well, and so did Mary Linda Bell (thanks to encouragement from the Golden God). Mary Bell agreed with Ashley Sue that, so far as sex went, the woman did all the work, and Brother Simon got all the glory.

Oddly, it turned out that while Brother Simon's nasty words about me were clearly heard within the Cathedral, the *broadcast* audio was completely silent while he was trash-talking me. Combine that with all the problems with the video picture, and not even lip-readers knew what Brother Simon had said. Whereas 99 percent of what his wife said, went out over the air as clear as a bell.

Brother Simon had warned his wife that if she went off his Contriteness script, there would be a divorce, and then there would be starvation. Brother Simon's prediction came true, but not the way he'd predicted—

For some reason, Mary Bell got the idea that she had to show a local newspaper photographer the shredder where Brother Simon shredded prayer-requests without reading them. Divine Blessings Cathedral got zero contributions after that, till the elders fired Brother Simon.

Eventually Brother Simon got a job as a gardener in a retirement home in Boise, Idaho.

Meanwhile, I had discovered that I couldn't go anywhere in town without teenage girls—and their mothers!—looking at me with interest.

Two girls from Ewert Grant High School's chess club invited me to speak at their school for Career Day. They both lost their virginity to me fifth period, on the teacher's desk in Biology Class.

Chapter 19
The Last Puzzle Piece

My adventure at Divine Blessing Cathedral had happened on a Sunday. (Duh.) Just under a week later—actually, sometime between midnight and dawn of the following Sunday—my bedside phone rang.

Sarah was terrified. "Duke is outside the club and he's acting crazy! He's got a baseball bat, and he says he'll bash my brains out when I step outside!"

I looked at the bedside clock. It was 2:13.

I said into the phone, "So call the cops, honey."

"George did. The cops told him, it could take forty-five minutes or an hour before they get here. Cops get busy when the bars close on Saturday night."

"Then lock the doors and stay inside, Sarah."

"We are, George and I. But I'm so *scared*, Tim honey."

I did the math. As far as I could tell, Duke and his baseball bat couldn't get into the Nimfo Club building. Meaning, Sarah was in no danger—*if* she stayed put. But if the cops showed up and Duke didn't put down his bat, the cops would have to shoot him like a rabid dog.

What the math also told me was that if Duke died, it was because of something I'd done: becoming Sarah's boyfriend through my Power. Admittedly, I'd done that without meaning to. Still, it meant I had a responsibility to defuse tonight's crisis and keep Duke alive, if I could.

"I'm leaving for Nimfo," I said, and hung up. I stopped only long enough to scribble a note for Slave Deborah, and to get dressed. Then I was zooming.

As I was yawning and driving through the blackness, it occurred to me: Duke likely wouldn't see me as the man who was going to save him from death by cop-bullet—nope, he'd see me as the man who stole his girlfriend. What I was doing was noble, but it sure wasn't smart.

Still, I kept driving toward the Nimfo Club.

It was easy to figure out that I was seeing Duke. Tall with a gymnasium build and a blond crew cut, I would have known him even without his MLB equipment. As I cut the engine, Duke was using his bat to beat on a reinforced-steel door. When I cut my headlights, Duke glanced in my car's direction. Once he figured out that he wasn't looking at a cop car, his attention returned to the door.

"SARAH, YOU GET YOUR WHORE ASS OUT HERE *RIGHT NOW*! THE MORE YOU MAKE ME WAIT, THE WORSE YOU'RE GONNA HURT LATER!"

There was a pause of several seconds, then—

"DON'T GIVE ME THAT SHIT! YOU'RE *MY* GIRL, GOT IT?"

I hope my Power is up to the challenge! I thought. Then I stepped out of my car and walked toward the man who was swinging his bat like a fire ax.

When I got close to him, I said, "You don't need to do that. There are billions of other women in this world."

He whirled around, surprised. Then he said, "Buddy, this isn't your pr—"

Then he *looked* at me, and said, "Ain't I lucky, just the man I want to see. You bullshitted my girlfriend, and your dad sold my grandpa a piece-of-shit Pinto. Now it's payback time."

Duke started walking toward me.

As soon as he was moving my way, I said, "Duke, stop. Calm down." I tried to keep my own voice calm.

Duke kept coming, and his furious expression didn't change. Clearly my on-again, off-again Power hadn't worked.

"Let's talk about this, Duke," I said. It sounded lame, even to me.

"You're good at talk. I'm good at muscles. I'm done talking," Duke replied.

I stood my ground, even knowing this was perhaps a fatally stupid choice. But before things could get nasty—the steel-reinforced door opened. And quickly shut again.

Duke turned his back on me and ran toward the door, his bat held high. Then he stopped.

"Please don't hit me, I'm not her!" an alto voice said.

The red-haired stripper Sunset was staring at Duke and his bat, utterly terrified.

"Come with me," Duke said.

"Please, it's late, I need to go home," Sunset said.

"I'm not gonna hurt *you*," Duke said. "I just want you to see something."

"Please let me leave, I won't tell anyone—"

"Sweetie, you're beginning to piss me off."

Her shoulders sagging, Sunset walked with Duke over to me. I had not moved, except to pick up a two-foot-long two-by-four that had been laying on the pavement.

Duke said, "Aw look, the boy's got a board. Sweetie, I want you to tell Sarah what you see and what you hear. In a minute, he's gonna start begging."

Then Duke turned to me and stepped forward. I retreated. While stepping back, I planted my foot on a beer bottle. The bottle rolled, my foot rolled with it, and I lost my balance—just as Duke swung for my head. I got hit, and it was no picnic, but it wasn't the concussion (or worse) that Duke had intended. But when I fell down, the two-by-four went flying.

Duke moved up to my body that was flat on the ground; he brandished the bat. But he didn't swing it down—I guess he wanted to savor the moment. Maybe he really was hoping that I'd beg for my life.

No way. I called out, "Sunset, pick up the board, and throw it to me!"

She looked panicked at my words. And when Duke turned around, looked into her eyes, and shook his head, she looked ready to wet herself.

"Tsk," he said to me, "asking a cunt for help. Not manly at all."

My next words slipped out: "Robert, hit him with the board! ROBERT!"

Duke didn't even bother to look around. "The bouncer's name is *George*. There's no 'Robert' out here, just a couple of *pussies*."

That's when Sunset smacked him upside the head. Hard. He instantly went to sleep.

She dropped the board, looking panicky again. "Oh my god, why did I hit him? And how did you know that I was, that I was— *Who told you?*"

I didn't tell Sunset why she'd hit him. But at last, I myself knew why she'd done it, because at last I figured out what my gift was.

'Susan', 'Sarah', 'Ashley', and 'Robert'—those were the real names of people. 'Susie', 'Platinuma', 'Gothika', and 'Sunset'— those were false names. When I spoke to someone by a false name, nothing special happened. But when I spoke to someone—including myself—by their real name, they believed my statements, answered my questions, and obeyed my commands.

'Duke' was also a false name. Which meant—

I knelt down next to unconscious Duke and began fishing for his wallet. Sunset, meanwhile, was still looking at me, needing answers to her questions.

I said, "Robert, be calm. Sarah told me about your surgery, and that you can't yet afford to go to name-change court. But believe me, Robert, nobody who looks at you can tell that you used to be a guy. Trust me with your secrets, Robert."

Sunset actually smiled at that. Meanwhile, I had just opened Duke's wallet.

"Francois Duquesne"? Duke's real name is "Francois Duquesne"? No wonder he uses an alias!

"So what happens now?" Sunset asked calmly. "The police supposedly will be here soon."

"That's a good question," I said. Then I looked into Duke's face and said, "Francois Duquesne, wake up."

Duke's eyes opened. "What happened?"

"Tell me the last things you remember, Francois."

"I was gonna hit you with my bat, then you told the cunt to throw you the board, but I set her straight. Then you told 'Robert' to hit me, and wham! So who's Robert?"

"Oh, *shit*!" Sunset said.

I said, "Francois, forget all about Robert, forget any mention of Robert. Francois Duquesne, here's what happened: I was lying on the ground after you hit me. I'd dropped the two-by-four. She"—I gestured at Sunset—"said that she was going back inside and give the police another call. You turned around and walked after her, intending to hit her. Doing that, you turned you back on me and the two-by-four, and then you got hit."

"Damn, *that* was stupid of me." He started to get up. "This time, I'll be smarter."

A police car drove up.

To Duke I said, "There won't be a 'this time.' " To Sunset I said, "Go tell the cops that Duke and I had a fight. Then go tell George and Sarah to come outside." Then I said to Sunset very quietly, "Robert, do *not* mention that it was you who hit Duke. Trust me to handle this."

Sunset in her purple stilettos walked over to the police car.

Thirty minutes later, Duke was handcuffed and in the back seat of that police car, which was driving away.

The two arresting officers had a firm belief that Sunset was involved only as a witness. (I *know* they had an undoubting belief in Sunset's innocence, because I put that belief into their heads.)

Meanwhile, George the bouncer was pumping my hand, and had just given me a hard slap on the back. Sarah was crying, and was waiting for George to let go of me, so that she could throw her arms around me.

And Sunset? She was looking at me in wonder: *How did you keep me out of jail?*

I was feeling wonder myself. *I've been given Power to control minds, and now I know how the Power works.*

Something caught my eye. Standing in a corner of Nimfo Club's parking lot was a bald-headed man wearing a white shirt and blue tie. He was too far away, and that part of the parking lot was so dark, that I couldn't tell if his blue tie had white polka dots.

When he saw me looking at him, the man smiled, gave me two thumbs up, then vanished.

THE END

Find out about Doctor MC's previous novels and stories, and read free sample chapters, at:
http://doctormcmadscientist.wordpress.com/about/

Find out about Doctor MC's upcoming fiction, and read free sample chapters, at:
http://doctormcmadscientist.wordpress.com/

If you liked this story: **Please go to its Amazon page and write a five-star review. Thank you.**

www.ingramcontent.com/pod-product-compliance
Lightning Source LLC
Chambersburg PA
CBHW051259170626
46809CB00004B/1715